"Hey, what are you doing?" asked Little Brother, coming into the workshop.

He saw the empty workbench. Empty, that is, of food. Something was going on here for sure! "Aren't you hungry? Want me to fix something to eat?"

Burton shook his head. He scarcely heard the question. Food was the last thing on his mind. "You never saw such sad kids," he said. "I've got to get this ready to use now. Right now."

Little Brother's eyes widened. "But you haven't tested it," he protested. "You can't just use it on people without testing it! If it doesn't work the way you think it will . . . I mean, what if there's an accident and somebody gets hurt? I mean, you don't really know what will happen."

"That's right," said Burton. "So I'm going to test it. Right now. On me."

Books by Dorothy Haas

Burton's Zoom Zoom Va-Rooom Machine
Burton and the Giggle Machine

Published by MINSTREL Books

Dorothy Haas

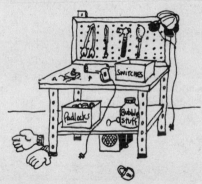

A MINSTREL® BOOK

Published by POCKET BOOKS

New York   London   Toronto   Sydney   Tokyo   Singapore

This book is a work of fiction. Names, characters, places and incidents are products of the author's imagination or are used fictitiously. Any resemblance to actual events or locales or persons, living or dead, is entirely coincidental.

A Minstrel Book published by
POCKET BOOKS, a division of Simon & Schuster Inc.
1230 Avenue of the Americas, New York, NY 10020

Text copyright © 1992 by Dorothy F. Haas
Illustrations copyright © 1992 by Cathy Bobak

Published by arrangement with Bradbury Press

ISBN: 0-671-79897-9

First Minstrel Books printing January 1996

10 9 8 7 6 5 4 3 2 1

A MINSTREL BOOK and colophon are registered trademarks of Simon & Schuster Inc.

Cover art by Dan Burr

Printed in the U.S.A.

For Ellen,
who so often
shares my amusement

Contents

1

The Va-ROOOM Machine

*B*urton lifted his face to the passing breeze. The cool morning air brushed his cheeks. Under his feet, the va-ROOOM machine rolled smoothly over the sidewalk. He sighed with pleasure. There was nothing like an early morning spin in the park before curious people began cluttering up the place.

Okay. Now for something more. He tapped a button on the small box in his hand.

A soft sputter sounded underfoot. A gentle hiss followed as the va-ROOOM machine's rockets kicked in.

It picked up speed, lifting at a gentle angle. He leveled off, skimming above the shrubbery that lined the walkway. He grinned. Nice! Was this, he wondered, how birds felt when they slipped up and down the air currents?

He moved along in a straight line, past the drinking fountain, past the shuttered snack bar. Over to his left he glimpsed the statue of Hans Christian Andersen sitting in a thoughtful pose looking at a book on his knee. How about a friendly greeting to Mr. Andersen?

Again he fingered the controls. Wings slid out on either side of the va-ROOOM machine. Power flowed from the magnetic shoe grips. He felt his shoes clamp tightly onto the deck. Ready? Action!

He banked to the left, soaring up and over a cluster of benches and continuing on in a smooth curve. "Morning, Mr. Andersen," he sang out as he passed the bowed figure.

Hans Christian Andersen did not answer. Of course. But a small figure crouched in the shadows of a nearby bush had something to say. "Ha!" muttered Professor Savvy. His eyes were not on Burton but on the amazing machine he rode. "Hoo-hee! The lad's invention is indeed astonishing."

Glumly he watched Burton skim up and over the slide in the playlot and circle around the swings.

"Drat Miss Doyle," grumbled the professor. His ears

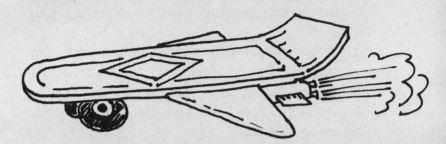

twitched. "Drat her for making me promise I would not take anyone's invention."

Miss Doyle was Burton's teacher. Once, long, long ago, she had been Professor Savvy's teacher, too. Not so long ago she had forced, *forced,* him to write on the chalkboard a hundred times, "I will never, never take anyone's invention ever again." That had happened on the day he almost—but not quite—made off with the va-ROOOM machine. Memories of that sad day still made him turn an interesting shade of pea green.

Grumpily, he huddled in the shadows . . . thinking . . . thinking . . . thinking. . . . Hoo. Ha. Hee.

Burton came sailing back past the statue, heading for home. As he neared the entrance to the park, he shut down the rockets. The wings slid out of sight. The magnets eased their grip on his shoes. He glided to a stop on the cement walk. Time to quit. People were beginning to appear on the street—among them Little Brother bringing Clinton to the park for his morning run.

Little Brother spotted Burton. As he came near, his eyes went from Burton's face down to the va-ROOOM machine and back up to Burton's face. "Hey! I thought you were still asleep," he said. He looked around. "Did anyone see you?"

Burton shook his head. "Nobody comes to the park this early." He tucked the va-ROOOM machine under his arm and turned back into the park to keep Little Brother company while Clinton nosed around among the trees.

"Listen, Burt," said Little Brother. "I've been thinking about something. I don't know if it'll work, but it's worth a try. Do you still have the drawings you made when you were inventing the va-ROOOM machine?"

"Yep." Burton nodded. "Matter of fact, I was going to toss them out today. It's time to clean out the workshop and get to work on something new."

"Can I have them?" asked Little Brother.

"Well, sure," Burton said good-naturedly. "But why? What're you planning on doing with them?"

"Oh, something," Little Brother said vaguely. "I'll tell you about it if it works. But look, there's another thing." He spoke seriously. "Do you suppose you

4

could keep the va-ROOOM machine under wraps for a while yet?"

"You mean not take it out at all?" Burton couldn't believe what he was hearing. "Aw, come on! That's asking a lot. It's the best thing I ever invented."

"Yeah, it is," Little Brother agreed. "But what I'm thinking is, what if Professor Savvy ambushes you? He might just take it! He could—"

"Hey," said Burton. "How? He isn't a whole lot bigger than me. I'd put up a fight. And anyway, I don't think he'll do that, not after the talking-to Miss Doyle gave him. She made him promise, you know, and so I—"

"I know, I know," said Little Brother. "A promise is a promise. You keep 'em. I do, too. So does everyone we know. But him? I don't know. So—just for a while? Will you keep it out of sight? Will you, huh?"

"How long is *a while*?" asked Burton.

"I'm not sure." Little Brother bit his lip, thinking. "But it can't be for too long. And I'll tell you as soon as it's okay."

Burton thought about it. Little Brother usually had good reasons for whatever he did. "Okay." He sighed. "But I hope you know what you're asking."

The worried frown on Little Brother's face melted. "Thanks, Burt. You won't be sorry. I mean, I think you won't be." He looked around. "Clint?" he yelled.

"Where are you?"

"Yip!"

Little Brother spied Clinton sitting under a tree near the Hans Christian Andersen statue, looking up into the leaves.

"Aw, come on, Clint," yelled Little Brother. "Leave that squirrel or whatever's up there alone. Hurry up or we'll be late for breakfast."

Saturday breakfasts were special in the Knockwurst house. Mama insisted that nobody miss them.

Clinton didn't turn. He didn't come.

"Clinton?" Little Brother called in his no-nonsense voice. "You better come right now. If you don't, I'm going to go home and give your breakfast to Mitzi." Mitzi was the dog next door.

The threat touched Clinton. He looked over his shoulder at Little Brother.

"I mean it, Clint," called Little Brother.

With a last look upward into the leaves and a low growl that did not reach Little Brother's ears, Clinton came. Dragging his feet, pausing now and then to look back at the tree, he followed Burton and Little Brother home.

2
Robbers?

*B*urton stowed the va-ROOOM machine in the workshop and headed for the house. Little Brother said he'd be along in a minute—he wanted to check out the yard.

Burton's stomach growled. Breakfast time, and was he hungry! He could eat a moose!

Nose-tickling smells met him at the kitchen door. Mama was taking something out of the broiler. "Hurry, dears," she called, raising her voice to be heard throughout the house. "Our fritters are finished glazing."

Burton licked his lips and went to the sink to wash his hands. "What kind of fritters, Mama?" he asked over his shoulder.

"Pawpaw," she said. "I understand that pawpaws are good for inventive people. And certainly we are an inventive family." She remembered something. "Did you finish inventing your invention safe to protect our wonderful inventions?"

"All done." Burton dried his hands. "Finished it yesterday. It only needs the locks, and Little Brother said he'd get those today."

He followed Mama into the dining room. Papa and Big Sister Edisonia were just coming in from the hall. Papa was stepping majestically, humming a tune from his newest symphony. Edisonia was tap dancing, supplying a very pretty rhythm.

They took their places at the table and tucked their napkins into their collars. Little Brother came running. He slid into his chair just in time, before Papa started chewing. Clinton trotted in from the kitchen, carrying his empty bowl in his mouth. He set it down beside Little Brother's chair and waited, looking up at him soulfully.

Papa spooned the pawpaw fritters onto plates and passed them around the table. Mama dipped oatmeal-kumquat sauce onto the plates.

Burton nibbled. Yummy.

Little Brother put a couple of his own fritters and some sauce into Clinton's bowl. Clinton's eyes narrowed as he eyed his breakfast. He sniffed the fritters. He took a cautious nibble. Then he gobbled them up and waited for more.

The dining room was silent as everyone began to eat.

Little Brother broke the silence. "Someone was poking around out in the yard last night," he said matter-of-factly between bites.

Papa looked up, his fork in midair. "Poking around?"

"Robbers?" asked Edisonia.

Little Brother was reassuring. "Nobody can get in, of course. Not with Clinton patrolling the house. Right, Clint?"

"Grrr," growled Clinton.

Mama looked worried. "Are you sure, lovey?"

Little Brother winced. If only Mama would stop calling him babyish pet names! But he answered. He was sure. "There are footprints under the dining room window," he said, slicing off a piece of his next-to-last fritter for Clinton.

Heads swung toward the window. Nobody was outside looking in.

"My harp-flute!" gasped Edisonia. "Maybe someone wanted to steal it."

"My new symphony!" gasped Papa. "Could someone be after it, to claim it as their own work?"

"The new figures I worked out for the think tank!" gasped Mama. "Our national security could be in danger."

Only Burton was calm. He went right on eating. "I heard Clinton bark during the night," he said between swallows. "He scared whoever it was away."

"He's our first line of defense," said Little Brother.

Clinton stood up and shook himself, looking determined.

"There's something else to remember, too," Burton went on. "Even supposing somebody does want to break in and take our inventions, they won't be able to get them after today. From now on, we'll put them in the invention safe at night."

A great, gusting sigh of relief went around the table, and attention turned back to the pawpaw fritters. Who knew what good ideas they might all have today, after eating such special food for especially inventive people? Why, Little Brother got an idea while he was eating his second helping of fritters.

After breakfast he followed Burton out to the workshop. "You know, Burt," he said, "I've been thinking about the way Clinton patrols our house at night."

Clinton had settled down in a contented comma-curve at Burton's feet. Burton nudged his ribs with the toe of his shoe. "Nobody was ever safer than we are with you on the job, right, Clint?"

"Ar-roooo," agreed Clinton.

"No dog could do it better," said Little Brother.

Clinton lowered his eyes modestly.

"But I got this idea," Little Brother went on. "He's only got one growl."

"Huh?" The words grabbed Burton's interest. What was Little Brother getting at?

"Is there something . . ."—Little Brother looked off into the distance, trying to put his thoughts into words—"that could, well, sort of multiply his growl?"

Burton's eyes opened wide. He sat up straight, listening carefully, his mind darting around that idea.

"I mean," said Little Brother, "like if he growled at one window, is there some way other growls could come from other windows?"

"A whole army of growls," breathed Burton, getting excited.

"That sure would make robbers think twice about coming around here," Little Brother finished.

Burton was caught up by this startling idea. "Neat," he said softly. "Really neat."

Little Brother leaned on the workbench and watched as Burton began to doodle ideas on his sketch pad. Could a new invention be far behind? He hung around long enough to see the idea begin to grow. Then he took Clinton and headed for Popplemeyer's hardware store to find some good, strong locks for the invention safe.

3

Burton's Invention Safe

Burton was doing something with a transistor when Little Brother and Clinton came back from Popple-meyer's. "Got 'em," said Little Brother. He dumped a bagful of padlocks and jingling keys on the workbench in front of Burton.

Burton set aside the transistor. He picked up one of the locks and hefted it in his palm. "Heavy," he said approvingly. He tried the key. The padlock popped open. "Let's see how they fit," he said, getting up.

The invention safe stood at the back of the workshop, foursquare and solid. Made of metal that had once been part of a car—Burton had found the metal at an auto-body shop—it was too heavy for a robber or even two robbers to pick up and carry away. The corners were riveted. So were the sides. The door had security hinges. Rings in five places were waiting to take the padlocks.

Burton clipped the locks onto the rings. The invention safe was awesome.

"It's almost scary to look at," Little Brother said thoughtfully. "It looks kind of like a jail, only it's meant to keep people out instead of in."

"Yeah," said Burton, standing back and studying it. "It sort of tells you something important is inside. If anybody actually got into the workshop—"

"Hold it," said Little Brother. "I've got an idea." He dashed to the house. Minutes later he came back, a tablecloth draped over one arm. He carried a vase filled with daffodils from the yard. "This will make the invention safe look like something else," he said.

He tossed the tablecloth over the safe and set the vase on it. "What's that big word?" he asked. "You know—when you make something look like something else?"

"Camouflage," said Burton.

"Camouflage," agreed Little Brother. "Now it looks

14

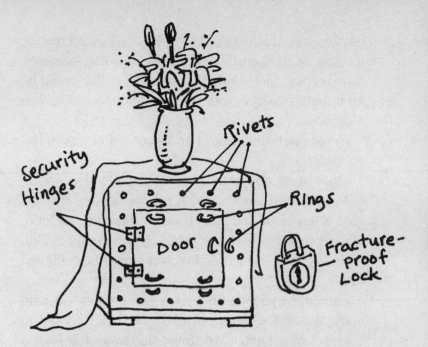

Security Hinges

Rivets

Rings

Door

Fracture-proof Lock

like a table. It sure does make the workshop look cozy."

That it did.

Burton went back to work on the transistor. But every now and then he glanced over at the "table" and grinned. He felt good knowing that his family's inventions were going to be safe.

He spent a busy day, working on the invention to multiply Clinton's growl. He had most of the things he needed right there in the workshop—bits of this and that he had picked up at garage sales. Hardly anything was shiny brand-new. But that didn't matter, as long as the things worked. He did not, however, have a collar that would fit Clinton. A collar would be an important part of this new invention. And that was a problem.

He emptied his pockets and counted his cash. Not enough.

On a shelf above the workbench stood a row of color-splashed paint cans. A purple-dripped can jingled when he picked it up. It was his garage sale fund. He emptied it onto the workbench and counted. Still, probably, not enough. There was only one thing left to do.

Pained, he robbed his bubble-gum ice cream fund and gave all the money to Little Brother. "Try not to spend it all," he said wistfully, thinking of at least a week without an ice-cream cone.

"I'll do my best," Little Brother promised. This was serious business.

He returned an hour later. "I did have to spend it all," he admitted. "I even had to add some of my money to it."

Burton felt terrible about that. Little Brother should not have to help pay for inventions. And besides, it might now take two weeks of no bubble-gum ice cream to catch up and pay him back. The thought brought on hunger pangs. He stroked the new collar, but it didn't take away the emptiness in his middle.

Little Brother guessed how he was feeling. "I'll get us a snack," he said, heading for the house.

He came from the kitchen with kohlrabi-squash shakes and Boston baked bean sandwiches—not ice cream, but they helped. Burton worked the rest of the day on the Clinton army. He didn't finish it, of course. But it was well on its way.

That night, as early evening darkness closed in around the Knockwurst house, a little parade emerged from the back door. It made its way to the workshop. Little Brother held the door open. Everybody entered. He followed them inside and closed the door.

"Hoo-hee," muttered a voice high in the butternut tree in the backyard. "What can this mean? My excellent instincts tell me something unusual is going on here."

17

Inside the workshop, Edisonia stowed the flute part of the harp-flute in the invention safe. The harp itself was too big to fit, of course. Papa put the music for his new symphony into the safe. Mama placed her notebook with all its national security figures in it on top of the sheaf of music.

"Little Brother must be feeling quite bereft," she said softly to Papa, "not having an invention to keep safe."

"Patience, my love," murmured Papa. "Little Brother's day will come."

Little Brother didn't feel the least bit bereft. He watched, pleased, as his family placed their valuable inventions in safekeeping.

Burton put the va-ROOOM machine in the invention safe, of course. He could not, however, lock up his automatic dog washer and his no-hands automatic bed-making machine. They were too big to take apart each night and put together again each morning. They were going to have to take their chances with robbers.

Everybody oohed and aahed over the invention safe as Burton put the locks in place and snapped them— *click!*—shut—*click!*—one by one. *Click click click!* Little Brother put the tablecloth over the invention safe and set the daffodils in place. Then the little parade left the workshop. Little Brother fastened the extra big, supertough padlock on the door, and they returned to the house.

The leaves of the butternut tree shook. They shivered. They quivered. "Hoo!" muttered the voice from the top of the tree. "Hee! Something is indeed going on here. My curiosity is beginning to bubble. But I will not let it get out of hand. I will move slowly. Events will reveal what I must know before I act."

4

Clinton's Army

Certain that their inventions were safe, the Knock-wursts slept like tops that night. The next morning, after they took them out of the safe, Little Brother looked around the yard. There was no trampled grass, no footprints, no sign of anyone having prowled about the place during the night. He didn't expect there to be, though, because Clinton hadn't let out a sound from dusk to dawn.

Turning Clinton into an army was a great idea, but not a simple one. It took Burton the rest of the day to finish the growl multiplier. Transistors were part of it, and batteries, and minispeakers and such. The On-Off switch was remote, hand held. He fixed the collar Little Brother had bought so that it fit comfortably around Clinton's neck and set up the speakers in different places around the house.

Little Brother trotted after him, handing him tools as they were needed. "Is it done now?" he asked when Burton had the laundry room speaker in place.

"Mmm," Burton said absentmindedly, counting off the number of speakers on his fingers.

"Ready for the big test, boy?" Little Brother asked Clinton, who had trailed after him. He knelt and hugged him.

Clinton licked Little Brother's ear.

Burton wasn't listening. He stood looking around, biting his lip, thinking. Something still remained to be done. But what? Something that would expand the area of protec—The "something" popped up and, you might say, socked him. Of course! The workshop! That needed protection, too! He headed for the workshop, hastily put together another speaker, and mounted it under the workbench.

"Now?" asked Little Brother. "Now can we test it?"

"Now," said Burton, leading the way back to the house. "We'll test in short bursts," he explained. "We don't want to upset the neighbors."

Inside, he touched the On switch and showed Clinton a picture of something that always brought out the worst in him—a rabbit.

Clinton growled. The growl multiplied. Growls came from the living room . . . the dining room . . . the basement . . . the front and back halls . . . and the workshop. For a moment, the Knockwurst place was alive with growls. Burton cut the sound short.

Clinton looked surprised. Warily, he looked around him.

Burton tapped the On switch just as Clinton let out a yip.

Yips came from all sides.

A worried furrow appeared between Clinton's eyes. He looked baffled, confused.

Little Brother led him around the house, showing him all the speakers.

Clinton caught on quickly, and it didn't take him long to get used to the growl multiplier. When he growled and heard growls coming from every direction, his head went up and his chest puffed out. He looked for all the world like a four-star general. General Clinton, in charge of all those fierce noises.

Burton grinned. There was nothing like a good invention to lift the spirits, no-sirree!

"Burr-tonn? Oh, Burton!"

The call came from the backyard.

Burton opened the door. His friends Jonathan and Tish were standing there, looking puzzled. Kevin came whizzing around the corner of the house on his skateboard to join them.

"Sounds like you turned your house into a dog day camp," said Jonathan.

"Is Clinton jealous of all those dogs?" asked Tish. She was cuddling her new puppy, Punker.

"What's going on?" asked Kevin.

Burton went outside and joined them. The growl

multiplier had to be secret. Word must not get out that Clinton was still patrolling the place by himself. "Clinton isn't the least bit jealous," he said offhandedly. Which was the truth. "I'm just experimenting," he added.

His friends exchanged glances. Burton was up to something. They knew they weren't going to find out anything more until he was good and ready to tell them what he was working on.

"We're heading over to the Big Freeze for ice cream," said Tish. "Want to come?"

"Well, sure," Burton started to say. Then he remembered the sad shape of his funds. What funds? His funds were zilch! "Uh, look," he said, "I've got to pass today. There's stuff I have to do in the workshop."

He didn't fool anybody. "Broke, huh?" Jonathan said sympathetically.

"Broke," Burton admitted.

"Maybe none of us should go," said Tish. "Why don't we just hang out here and keep Burton company?"

Burton wouldn't let them do that. It was bad enough that he wasn't going to have any ice cream for a long time to come. No need to make his friends suffer with him.

He watched them head off for the Big Freeze, then went into the house to find out what the freezer held.

What it held was a papaya pop. He found it under

a package of frozen pattypan squash. Good. But not as good as bubble-gum ice cream.

The glow of having finished a new invention stayed with him for the rest of the day and through the night, too. He dreamed a good dream, about walking through a forest with inventions growing on the trees. Each invention whispered, "Pick me," as he passed. He woke up still feeling good, although he couldn't remember any of the inventions that wanted to be picked.

The night had passed quietly. Clinton had not let out a single bark, and so that meant nobody had been skulking around the yard.

Burton went off to school still feeling good. Monday morning. A brand-new week. Who knew what it held for him?

5

Trouble, Trouble, Everywhere

*W*ho indeed! The day started on a high, but it slid rapidly downhill.

Tish and Jonathan and Kevin were waiting for him at the corner. Tish was wearing one red sneaker and one yellow one and looking worried. "Punker did this to me," she moaned. "He chewed up the mates to these shoes. My mom said shoes don't grow on trees and I'll have to wait awhile for another pair."

It was, then, going to be a red-and-yellow shoes month for Tish. Awful! She was downhearted. Burton and the others said comforting things, but something of her mood rubbed off on them as they walked to school.

When the bell rang and they filed into their class-room, Miss Tilly Doyle stood watching them, her arms folded. "Is everyone ready for a challenge?" she boomed in her usual hearty way, looking around as they settled down at their desks.

Uh-oh! Miss Doyle's challenges as often as not spelled work—lots of hard, unending work. Somebody groaned.

Miss Doyle's head snapped up. She looked around. "Don't tell me," she roared, "that somebody here is afraid of challenge! Where is your mettle, your cour-age?"

Nobody spoke.

She picked up a stack of envelopes from her desk. "We," she boomed, "are about to embark upon a new class project." Moving swiftly up and down the aisles in her cloudhoppers, the Hovercraft shoes Burton had invented for her, she handed out the envelopes. "In these envelopes," she said, "are directions for different kinds of things. Each of you will make the thing or things described."

Burton ripped open his envelope. Inside was a card. "Make eight arcs," it said, and it told how long they were to be, and how thick, and how high the humps

in the middle were to be. He looked up, bewildered. "But what is the project? What are we making?"

"That," boomed Miss Doyle, "is for me to know and you to find out."

"But," stuttered Burton, "but—but—" He looked around. Puzzlement was written on every face in the room. "But how can we make something if we don't know what we're making!"

Miss Doyle smiled. "It's all part of the challenge," she said, "part of the game."

Some game! Was one side—Miss Doyle's—to have all the answers and the other side none?

"I don't want you people to just *do* things." Miss Doyle was suddenly serious. "I want you to think, and to have fun doing it. Won't it be fun to dig out the answer for yourselves?"

"No!" The word rippled through the room.

Miss Doyle ignored it.

"You may ask questions," she went on. "You will find your answer in my replies. Add them up. That will be much more fun than simply being told to do something."

Fun? Ha!

"Your questions?" She stood there, looking around, waiting, her cloudhoppers hissing softly in the quiet room.

Nobody spoke. Nobody had the least idea where to begin.

"Since you have no questions," Miss Doyle said after a moment, "we will just get on with our handwork. Each of you will make a drawing of the thing or things you are to make."

And so Burton settled down to draw arcs that were to be part of . . . who knew what?

It was a long, hard day. Trouble was in the air. Tish, of course, already had her trouble. It didn't take long for Kevin and Jonathan to find theirs.

Kevin got into trouble after lunch when Miss Doyle caught him retying the loop on his lariat instead of doing his math workbook pages. He got a good talking-to and had to write about not tying knots in ropes a hundred times.

The afternoon was almost over when Jonathan got into his trouble. Miss Doyle discovered that he was reading about famous spies in his library book rather than rewriting his book report.

Miss Doyle kept the spy book. She gave Jonathan a good talking-to, about how school was necessary to help him prepare for his future.

"What good will a book about superspies do Miss Doyle?" he demanded later as they walked home from school.

What indeed? Nobody had an answer for him.

Everybody had troubles. And what's more, they still had Miss Doyle's challenge to think about.

"Burt, you're good at working out problems," said Tish. "Can you figure out what we're going to build?"

But Burton was as baffled as everybody else. He had thought about the new class project all afternoon. "I've got to make eight arc things," he said. Suddenly he remembered their size. "They've got to be six feet long and one of them has to hump up three feet in the middle. So whatever we're making, it will be big." That was a clue of sorts.

"Slab things," said Kevin. "That's what I've got to make." He dug his drawing out of his backpack and studied it. "They kind of look like the tiles on our roof," he added.

"Mine are rods," said Tish. She showed them her drawing. "They've got hooks on the ends," she pointed out.

30

Jonathan studied the drawing. "Hey, mine are rods, too. Only mine have got loops on them. Do you suppose your hooks fit into my loops?"

Burton was still thinking about slabs, slabs that looked like roof tiles. "Do you suppose we're going to make some kind of house?" he wondered. "You know, like maybe an igloo?" Igloos were made of slabs.

"Or something that goes?" asked Kevin. Suddenly he looked more cheerful. Anything that moved, the faster the better, lightened Kevin's heart. "Let me see those rods. Cars have rods, you know, and—"

His words were cut off by the rumble of skate wheels bearing down on them at top speed. "Greetings, crawlers," a familiar voice called from behind them.

They groaned. Only one person in the world made that much noise and announced himself that way. Merrill Frobusher. Sighing, they stepped off the sidewalk so as not to be run down.

But Merrill did not speed past them as he usually did. He swung around and skidded to a stop in front of them. He eyed Kevin's skateboard and then looked around. "How're you guys doin'?"

Stunned silence met the question. Merrill, for once, sounded like a halfway real person. Where were his usual insults? Was he sick or something?

"Uh, great," said Burton, answering for all of them.

31

"Listen, Knockwurst, uh, I mean Burt," said Merrill, sounding a little less sharklike than usual, "how come I never see you out skateboarding? I mean, you've got that terrific skateboard with rockets and all. Why don't we get together and board around town sometime? Might be fun."

For some reason, Burton didn't want to explain about his promise to Little Brother. "Yeah," he said vaguely. "Might be. Maybe sometime." What else could he say? Merrill was offering to be friendly, and when people try to be nice, it's only polite to be nice back to them. Even if you don't like them. Maybe especially if you don't like them, because it's easy enough to be polite to people you like.

"Well, see ya," said Merrill, pushing off. He flicked a wave at them over his shoulder as he headed down the street.

"He sure knows how to ride that thing," sighed Kevin. "Wow, does he build up speed."

"Why is it I don't trust the guy?" asked Jonathan. "Burt, I don't know whether you should pass on that invitation or go along with it to find out if he's up to something."

Nobody answered, nobody moved, as they watched Merrill weave in and out among the people on the street.

Someone else watched, too. Someone hidden

32

among the bushes in the parkway that divided the street, someone who had been following Burton and his friends.

"Hoo-hee," murmured Professor Savvy, his eyes on the figure disappearing in the distance. "Now there is someone worth knowing. Yes indeedy. I just might have use for that boy. I think I will have a talk with him."

6 _____

More Trouble

Burton's feeling that the week would hold wonderful things faded as the week wore on.

Bad things didn't actually happen to him. The mood around the house was upbeat. Nobody tried to break in. That was clear, for Clinton and his army never let out a yip. The inventions were safe. Papa and Mama and Edisonia stopped worrying about robbers. Burton felt good about that. But his friends—they were another story. Burton was a caring sort of person. When his friends felt terrible, he felt terrible, too.

Kevin met him at the corner on Tuesday looking

grim. He waved a slip of orange paper. "It's a ticket," he moaned. "A police officer on Aspidistra Drive said I was speeding on my skateboard yesterday afternoon. I have to go to kids' traffic court."

Now that was trouble with a capital *T*.

"What do you suppose they do to kids at traffic court?" he wondered.

"My dad got a ticket once," said Jonathan. "That was for grown-ups' court. He had to pay a fine."

Kevin turned pale. "How much? I haven't got a lot of spare cash."

Jonathan didn't know. They went on to school feeling far from chipper.

The day after that, Tish met them with more bad news. She held out a book. "Look what Punker did," she wailed.

Burton winced. The back cover looked as though it had gone through a meat grinder.

"And what's more," Tish went on, "he ate the last page, too. Now I'll never know how it ends. And what am I going to tell Miss Puccini?" Miss Puccini was the librarian. A chewed-up book is one of the things librarians do not like. Definitely. No chewed-up books.

It was hard to find something comforting to say to Tish. Jonathan tried. "How about sprinkling something on paper stuff to make Punker back off? Like, well, how about some pepper?"

Tish was uncertain. "I don't think that would be

good for a puppy. It might hurt him. I'll think of something," she said bleakly. "I've got to." She went on ahead of them to get to school and face Miss Puccini before class. Her feet in their red and yellow sneakers dragged.

She was waiting on the steps when they got to school. "Miss Puccini was pretty nice," she said. "I have to pay for the book, as much as I can. And I have to help her in the library someday after school."

So maybe things weren't so bad?

"Only, how can I do that," she worried, "when I have to go right home after school to keep Punker from chewing up the house?"

Burton didn't have an answer. Nobody did. One problem just seemed to lead to another.

And then there was the class project, still that to think about. Miss Doyle didn't give in. She kept telling them she wanted them to have fun—fun!—figuring out what they were going to make. But their questions didn't bring any helpful clues to "add up."

"Is it something that goes?" asked Kevin.

"Well"—Miss Doyle was thoughtful—"not now," she said finally.

Kevin's face lit up. "Then it used to go! Did it go fast? Are we making an old-time race car?"

"Try another line of questions, boy," roared Miss Doyle. "You are far from the answer."

"If it's something that used to go," said Tish, "it isn't a vegetable."

"What are you asking, girl?" demanded Miss Doyle.

"Vegetables don't move around," said Tish. "So is it an animal or a mineral?"

"Both," said Miss Doyle. "Animal *and* mineral."

The room was still. That could not be. Animals lived and walked around. Minerals just lay around waiting for people to find them.

"No fair," muttered Kevin.

"What did you say?" Miss Doyle looked daggers at Kevin.

"Er," stuttered Kevin, thinking fast, "no hair?" *Hair* sounded like *fair*.

Miss Doyle relaxed. "No hair," she said.

"If it hasn't got hair, maybe it's got feathers," said Tish.

"Or maybe scales," said Jonathan.

"Well, at least we know it's not an igloo," said Burton, remembering the slabs Kevin was making.

"Igloo!" roared Miss Doyle. "Igloos are not animals. Didn't I say it was animal and mineral?"

"Yes, ma'am," said Burton. "I was only thinking out loud. But if it hasn't got hair, maybe it's a bird or a fish." He was really puzzled. "Only those are animals, not minerals."

Miss Doyle had had enough. "You've had your clue

for today," she said. "Think about it." She beamed at them. "Isn't this fun?"

Nobody beamed back at her.

They got on with the work of the day.

Jonathan had other things than work of the day on his mind, though. He had just gotten interested in fingerprints. A spy ought to know how to tell one person's prints from another's.

He took his stamp pad with him to lunch, and everyone put their prints on a sheet of paper. He played fair. He didn't look while they did it.

Back in class, he got out his magnifying glass and began studying them. They were really very interesting. One had a little nick in it, as though the finger had been cut. Another had—

"Ahem!"

A shadow fell across Jonathan's desk.

"What," roared Miss Doyle, "have we here?"

Jonathan had another good talking-to, and Miss Doyle kept his magnifying glass.

After school, Burton stood in the driveway, watching his dispirited friends head for home. Their shoulders slumped. Their feet dragged. If only there was something he could do to help them. . . .

Still thinking, he stopped in the kitchen, put together a liverwurst and apple-butter sandwich, found a few pickles, and carried the snack out to the workshop. A gadget—some kind of machine would come in handy. Like now, when there were puppy troubles . . . kids' traffic court troubles . . . spy book and magnifying glass troubles. Something to give his friends a boost when trouble loomed. Funny. *Loom* rhymed with *gloom*.

He perched on his stool at the workbench, thinking, munching. Yum. Good sandwich. He bit into a pickle and felt his mouth pucker. Nice. Of course, a gadget couldn't make troubles go away. Sometimes people had to fix their own troubles. Or sometimes things had to change—the people around the trouble, or the place where the trouble was. Still, though, if there were some way to ease the misery while the trouble was happening . . .

He noodled ideas around in his head. He doodled them onto his sketch pad, thinking. He fingered pieces of a puzzle off to one side on the workbench, idly fitting pieces together, thinking. But nothing really worked out.

He sighed, wishing he could hurry things up in the idea department. But he knew he could not. Ideas grow in their own way and in their own time. They cannot be hurried.

7

Smoke Alert!

*T*he trouble roller coaster continued its downhill swoop.

Tish had more bad news the very next day. "Punker ate up my father's report," she said. "He had to stay up all night doing it over because his boss needs it first thing this morning."

Now that was superbig trouble. They all knew about reports and how Miss Doyle felt about them. A report for a boss had to be a thousand times worse.

"This morning Dad looked at Punker and said

maybe the country is the place for him where he can roam around and chew on everything he sees." Tish closed her eyes and shook her head. "Punker is the nicest thing that ever happened to me. Only now he's the worst, too."

Still talking about Punker, they turned into their classroom. They stopped dead in their tracks in the doorway. Stacks of cardboard sheets and bundles of cardboard tubes filled every bit of empty space in the room.

"Come in," roared Miss Doyle. "Don't just stand there gawking. You're causing a gridlock in the doorway."

True. Kids had bumped into Burton and the others and were hopping around behind them trying to see into the room.

Burton picked his way to his desk, in and out among the stacks and bundles, wondering what it all meant.

"We have work to do today, people," boomed Miss Doyle when everyone was seated. "Have you finished your drawings?"

Everybody had.

"Hold them up," she ordered.

Everybody did, and she went up and down the aisles, inspecting the drawings. "Good," she said here, and "Round your corners" there.

"Have you been adding up?" she asked, glancing around the room. "Have 'animal and mineral' led you to further questions?"

Burton had been thinking. "Does what we're making live in North America? Or someplace else?"

Miss Doyle was thoughtful. "You will find it," she said carefully, after a long pause, "on this continent."

That was some help. They could check out all the books on North American animals in the learning center.

Kevin had a question. "What's all the cardboard for?"

"Today we will begin construction," said Miss Doyle. "But not until later. Any more questions?"

Nobody could think of any.

"In that case," she boomed, "we will get on with our daily routine."

So they tended to their language arts and their social studies. And some of them worked on private projects.

Jonathan's grabber of the moment was his chemistry set. Miss Doyle had given him permission to bring it from home. He had not told her he was trying to make gunpowder—she might say he shouldn't—or that he had added to the chemicals in the set with odd bits of stuff he had picked up at the hobby shop.

He didn't work on gunpowder today, though. Tish's

troubles were on his mind. Could he maybe put together something that would help her train Punker not to chew up his surroundings?

He poured liquid from one jar to another and added a sprinkle of blue crystals. He shook it. It bubbled. To that he added a pinch of white powder and swirled the mixture around and around. He held it up to the light. He sniffed it. Pretty good.

He was not prepared for what happened next when he added drops of amber liquid from a small vial. Suddenly smoke billowed upward from the jar—horrible-smelling, choking, brown smoke.

The people around him backed away, coughing, gagging.

He should have jammed the lid back onto the jar in a hurry. He couldn't because tears were streaming down his cheeks and he couldn't see. The lid! The lid! Where was the darn thing? Blindly he pawed around on the table.

Wiping their eyes, holding their breath, everybody crowded into the hall. Unable to find the lid, Jonathan had no choice but to back away from the smoking jar and feel his way out of the room.

Mopping at her eyes, harrumphing and garrumphing, Miss Doyle headed for the office to get help. She bumped into Mr. Dedmun, the principal, coming into the hall to find out what the commotion was about.

Covering their mouths with their handkerchiefs, they shooed everyone outside into the open air and went to alert the other classrooms.

Outdoors, Jonathan began to see again. From where he stood with Burton, he watched the school custodian throw open the windows, set up fans to force the bad air out of the room, and flap wet towels to freshen the air.

Soon all the kids in school were milling around. They watched with excitement as a fire truck came thundering up the street and fire fighters trotted into the building.

What a hoot! They clapped Jonathan on the back and said friendly things like "Way to go!" and "Do this again, pal. Like tomorrow morning when we have our science test."

The time outdoors didn't last long enough. The fire fighters came back out of the building, climbed onto their truck, and rolled away. The kids gave them a big hand and the driver saluted back with an impressive *blawrrr* of his horn.

Miss Doyle shouldered her way through the crowd and shepherded them back into the building. "What," she roared as she stood aside to let them pass, "in the name of sound ecology were you doing, boy?"

Jonathan didn't have time to answer.

Mr. Dedmun was standing in the hall. "So that's the boy," he said, staring at Jonathan. He crooked a finger at him. Come . . . with . . . me, said that finger.

Shuddering, Jonathan went.

A long, long time later he came back into the room, gathered up his chemistry set, and went out again. Mr. Dedmun, it seemed, was about to become the owner of a wonderful chemistry set.

Jonathan came back in time to work on the group

project. He sliced away at his cardboard rods, making the loops bigger. But he did not have much to say. He looked sober, somber—in other words, miserable.

Burton had to do something. He just had to.

8

A New Invention— Maybe

*B*urton was deep in thought. He was not going to let his attention stray until he came up with something that would put some joy back into his friends' lives.

Hmm . . . Laughter . . . happiness . . . good feelings . . . What made those happen? Jokes? Jokes made people laugh. Even the terrible ones, the groaners, sort of made people feel good.

"Jokes," he wrote at the top of the page in his notepad. He doodled soap bubbles with smiling faces all around the word. Jokes. Yeah. Okay. But what else? His mind was blank.

Well, then, what was the invention going to look like? Would it be small—like a thing to wear on the wrist? Or like, maybe, something to wear in the ears? Probably best to start with something for ears, since jokes might be part of the machine.

He got to thinking of the punch lines of jokes, doodling while he thought. *It's been nice gnawing you. . . .*

A smile tugging at his lips, he sketched a cap sort of thing, thought for a moment, and added earflaps. The flaps could hold equipment.

Three lions and a scared zebra . . .

He grinned. He'd always liked that joke. He kept on drawing, outlining his hands. Still thinking, he took off his shoes and socks, put the sketch pad on the floor, and outlined his feet.

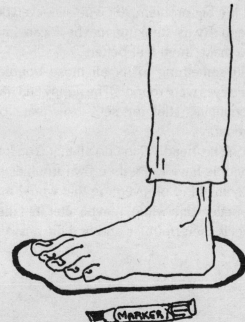

I don't know, but there's one standing right there behind you. . . .

With that one, he let out a guffaw.

"Hey! What're you doing, drawing your feet and laughing?"

It was Little Brother. He had come into the workshop unnoticed.

Burton chuckled again and repeated the punch line. "I don't know, but there's one standing right there behind you."

Without a pause, Little Brother said, "What do you call something with purple hair, a blue face, three eyes, and it's nine feet tall? Yuck yuck. Okay. But why are you standing there telling yourself jokes?"

While he pulled on his socks and shoes, Burton talked about the big problem. "So you see, everybody is gloomy, and I was thinking maybe I can invent something to make them feel better."

"You mean something to fix all those troubles?" Little Brother's eyes were round. "The puppy and traffic court and Jonathan's stink-um set?" Now that would be some invention!

Burton shook his head. "Can't do all that. You know how it is—people have to fix their own troubles. But if there was some kind of invention that would make the kids feel better for a while, maybe after that they'd be able to tackle their troubles and find the answers."

50

Little Brother did understand. "You'd be giving them a kind of vitamin pill. Can I help?"

But what could he do? Little Brother was not an inventor. Burton looked at him thoughtfully. He didn't like to discourage him when he offered to help.

"I know," said Little Brother. "For a start, how about some jokes nobody has heard? I can go to the library—"

"—and read all the latest gag books and fill me in," said Burton. "Great idea."

"You know," said Little Brother, "I think I'm going to like this invention even though I haven't got any troubles."

He headed out to the library, and Burton hunched back over his notebook, thinking . . . thinking. . . .

The only good thing that could be said for that week of woe was that it came to an end on Friday, with no more puppy or spy or speeding disasters. Of course, Tish did flunk her math test. And Jonathan did get a *T*—for "Terrible," Miss Doyle roared—on his report on chameleons. And Kevin did find out he had read the wrong book for the afternoon discussion about books.

"What are you going to do this weekend, Jon?" asked Tish as they ambled toward home.

"Write a new report about chameleons," said Jonathan. "Miss Doyle said there's more to chameleons than how they change colors to disguise themselves." He sighed. "I think that's the best thing about chameleons. What're you going to do?"

"Study for a new math test on Monday," said Tish. "And try to teach manners to Punker. How about you, Kev? Is this the Saturday you have to go to kids' traffic court?"

Kevin shook his head. "Next week. I'll read the book I missed. Miss Doyle said she would have a private talk with me"—he made a face—"first thing on Monday." Private talks with Miss Doyle were not something to look forward to.

"It's been such an awful week," sighed Tish. "We were jinxed. I'm not surprised I failed math."

Kevin, to his credit, did try to look on the bright side. "I'm one book ahead of you guys," he said. "I hope I'll remember all about it when we get around to talking about it. Hey, Burt, you're the only one of us who didn't get a special assignment for Monday. I guess you can spend the weekend sleeping, huh?"

"No way," said Burton. "I've got something going in the workshop." And he had the whole weekend to work on it. A good thing, too. He needed every minute he could get.

So intent were they on their troubles that they didn't even glance into the park as they passed it. If they had, they would have seen Professor Savvy and Merrill

Frobusher. The professor was talking, talking, talking. Merrill was listening, listening, listening. And nodding his head.

9

Midnight Skulkers

*W*ork on the invention speeded up when Burton didn't get sidetracked by everyday things like school. It began to shape up. It wasn't small, as he first thought it might be. It was big enough for a not-too-tall person to stand in. The person would plant bare feet on the footprint spot on the floor.

When Little Brother came in from the library late in the afternoon, Burton pointed. "Stand on those footprints, will you? Take off your shoes and socks first."

Little Brother did as he was told and waited, his eyes fixed on Burton.

Burton pressed a button.

The bottoms of Little Brother's feet tickled. He giggled and hopped off the foot spots.

Burton liked the sound of that giggle. "Good. Only you didn't stay there very long," he said, turning off the machine.

"Can't stand tickles on the bottom of my feet," said Little Brother.

"I'll have to do something about that," mused Burton. "Maybe some electronic gates to keep people from hopping out of the machine before it's done its work."

Little Brother sat on the floor and put on his socks and shoes. "Is foot tickling enough to make people feel good if they've been feeling bad?"

"It's not the whole answer," said Burton. "Just part. I've got ideas about other things, too. You'll see."

"I've got some good jokes for you," said Little Brother. "I'll tell you in a minute. But first I have to tell you about something I read in a science magazine. What it said was"—he gazed off into the distance, a faraway look in his eyes, seeing once more the exact words—" 'An unconfirmed report from the National Institute for Misery Control suggests that the misery effect arises out of the left side of the brain. Researchers have discovered that ris-ris-risibibble—' " He stuttered over the hard word.

"Spell it," said Burton, reaching for the dictionary he kept in a pigeonhole under the workbench.

"R-i-s-i-b-l-e," spelled Little Brother.

Burton flicked through the pages. "Here it is," he said. He pronounced it. "RIHZ-uh-bul. It means having to do with laughter."

"Well, why don't they just say laughter!" said Little Brother. He went on with the report. " 'Researchers have discovered that risible ions can be made to lock into misery proteins, thus neutralizing them.' " He spelled *neutralizing*.

"It means making them useless," Burton explained. "It's sort of like one minus one is zero."

"Is that something you can use?" asked Little Brother.

"Say it again," said Burton. "I want to be sure I've got it."

He listened, his forehead wrinkled in thought, as Little Brother repeated the report word for word. Little Brother's photographic memory was a wonderful help to Burton. "Yeah," he breathed softly, smiling. "I'm on the right track."

"And here's something else," said Little Brother. "I read it in another magazine. 'Scientists in Scandinavia report that sadness and happiness tend to build on themselves, increasing the effect. Once begun, the process is self-actualizing.' " He sighed. "I sure wish

I understood what all the big words mean."

"You will," Burton said comfortingly, "in another couple of years. What the reports mean is that scientists have found how people begin to feel happy or sad. The really important part is what you said last—that once people are happy or sad, they just get more that way. What the scientists didn't say was, why not give sad people a nudge in the other direction."

Little Brother let that soak in, frowning. The frown turned into a grin. "Like getting in an elevator and going up? You could go right through the roof, like a rocket."

"That would be a little much," said Burton. "All the kids need is a nudge in the up direction. Then maybe they'll be able to fix their problems. Now, what about those jokes you looked up?"

"Here's a good one," said Little Brother. "Why is that elephant on TV wearing pink ballet slippers?"

Burton, back to fiddling with the button that controlled the tickles, shook his head. "Dunno. Why?"

"Because she can't dance in pink tennis shoes," said Little Brother, laughing.

Burton joined in.

It was a good afternoon. The whole weekend was good. Little Brother trotted around after Burton, telling him jokes, watching him work.

Jokes and bubbles were part of the invention. Burton thought to include music when he became aware of sounds coming from the house—Edisonia practicing away at "Home on the Range." A mirror at the front of the invention added a lot, too. It would do peculiar things to the face of the looker. Cheeks would bulge. Eyes would shrink to dots. Noses would bend or bump up in the middle.

He added buttons to the control panel. The sign below one said PUSH WITH CARE. The other had just two letters, PB.

At last, on Sunday, he draped the machine with a sheet and they went into the house for things like homework—ugh!—and food—yum!—and bedtime—yawwwn.

That night, long after the Knockwurst house darkened, Clinton and his army set up a chorus of growls.

Burton, in the middle of a dream about a time machine, heard only dimly. He came awake just enough to be pleased that the growl multiplier was working so well and then let the time machine carry him away into the dreamy future.

Edisonia and Mama and Papa smiled in their sleep, comforted by knowing their inventions were safe with Clinton on patrol. They did not wake up.

Only Little Brother sat up at the sound, instantly alert. He slid out of bed and ran to the window just in time to see two not overly large figures dart from shadow to shadow and then slip away into the alley.

Clinton quieted down. So, too, did his army.

Little Brother knelt at his window, watching, waiting. But the dark figures did not return. In time his eyelids drooped. He slept, his head pillowed on his arms on the windowsill.

Clinton did not bark again that night.

Little Brother was troubled when he woke up the next morning. He stood up, stretching to get rid of the kinks from sleeping on the floor. Who was that wandering around out there in the yard last night? Not just one, but two people. Was there more he could do to keep his family safe? He headed off to school, his thoughts tangled up with the midnight skulkers.

Burton went off to school, his thoughts tangled up with the invention, the giggle machine. It was coming along nicely, but it still needed work. What was it that Little Brother had said about risible ions locking into misery proteins? Risible ions . . . risible ions. Where could he get some of those? Were they just floating around in the air waiting to be caught like butterflies in nets?

He went up the steps into school, not listening to Jonathan and Kevin and Tish talking, thinking about risible ions. And he went into his classroom, still thinking. Once you begin thinking about risible ions, it's very hard to think of anything else.

Class went on, a busy buzz in the background, as Burton thought.

Suddenly Miss Doyle's voice cut through the buzz. ". . . buzz . . . mumble . . . buzz . . . tell the class the most common means of transportation across the Sahara Desert? . . . Burton? . . . *Burton*!"

Burton looked up and said the first thing that came to mind. "Risible ions?" he said.

Miss Doyle's eyebrows shot up into her hairline. Her eyes bulged. "What in the name of common sense do risible ions—bits of matter charged with laughter— have to do with desert travel?"

"Uh," said Burton. "They make you forget how hot it is?"

"After school," Miss Doyle droned, "after school we will discuss why you were daydreaming about risible ions. For now, tell me about camels. *Camels*, Burton!"

10

Laughter in the Air

*O*ne of Papa Knockwurst's purple socks rose above the workshop roof. It stood straight out on a tall pole, filled with air. A thin tube led from the toe of this wind sock down into the workshop.

Inside, Burton was fastening the tube to the bottom of a big upside-down jug filled with water. As he made the connection, air from the wind sock bubbled into the jug and rose to the top, and water escaped from the bottom. When the whole jug was emptied of water, the jug would be filled with air from outdoors.

62

THE AIR COLLECTOR

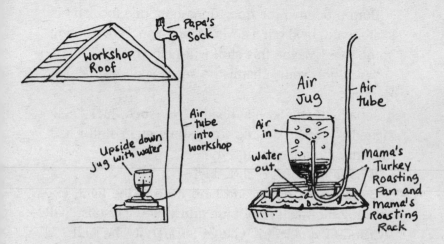

maybe, just maybe, that air would have risible ions in it. Maybe. Anything was worth trying.

Burton's skateboard leaned against the wall beside the door. It was the old skateboard, not the va-ROOOM machine. He was still keeping his promise to Little Brother not to use that for a while. He planned to go out on his board carrying another wind sock and head over to the park. Possibly he could capture some risible ions there. Lots of little kids played in the park, all of them laughing and squealing. There had to be lots of risible ions floating around the playground.

A knock sounded at the door. "Burt? You in there?" It was Jonathan.

Burton opened the door. Jonathan, one foot on his skateboard, held out a covered jar. "You were wanting some ions? Maybe this stuff will help you."

"You got your chemistry set back!" exclaimed Burton.

Jonathan shook his head. "No such luck." He sighed. "I mixed this up from some extra stuff I had at home. Wanna give it a try?"

What a friend! A real buddy!

Burton took the jar and held it up to the light, examining the mixture of blue and yellow crystals. "I'll try running an electric charge through it," he said. "It might be the final thing I need for the . . ." His voice trailed off as he thought of the things he still wanted to do with the invention.

"For the—" Jonathan prompted. But he didn't really expect an answer. He looked past Burton. A quite bulky something stood in the center of the room, covered with a sheet. No telling what it was. And what was that behind it? A table, with a checked tablecloth on it, and *flowers*? Burton sure was getting fancy!

Burton didn't answer Jonathan. "Uh, be with you in a sec," he said. He set the jar on the floor, picked up his skateboard and a tennis racket from which drooped another purple sock, and came out into the afternoon sunshine.

Little Brother appeared out of nowhere, a baseball cap tilted at a jaunty angle on the back of his head, Clinton trotting at his heels. "I'll lock up for you, Burt," he offered, snapping the padlock in place and giving it a couple of tugs to test it.

Kevin and Tish came swerving into the driveway on their skateboards. Tish was carrying Punker.

Kevin took in Burton's and Jonathan's skateboards. "Hey! You guys were going out. We can all go together."

Tish set Punker in the grass and sat down in the swing that hung from the butternut tree. "I think I'd better stay here," she said, beginning to swing. "Punker needs exercise."

"I'll stay with you," offered Little Brother. He meant to keep an eye on the workshop whenever he could. And the mail hadn't yet come. He could be here when it did, to check for letters addressed to him.

"Arf," barked Clinton. If Little Brother was going to stay, so would he. He went to investigate the funny little dog who had invaded his yard.

"Yip," barked Punker, to show he could hold his own if he needed to.

Burton rolled down the driveway on his skateboard.

So all right, he was earthbound, with the skateboard instead of the va-ROOOM machine. But, all the same, this outing could be fun.

Kevin rolled in an easy curving arc around him. He eyed the wind sock Burton carried. "Why have you got that purple sock fastened to that tennis racket?"

"Oh . . . it's for something for a . . . a . . ." Burton's voice faded.

Kevin shrugged. Oh well—nobody could blame a guy for trying!

They headed down Petunia Street, turned on Aspidistra Drive, crossed at the corner, and turned in at the west entrance of the park.

Merrill Frobusher rolled out of the shadows around the Hans Christian Andersen statue as they passed it. "Glad to see you're working out, Knockwurst," he said, gliding beside him. "Hey—what've you got there?" He pointed at the wind sock. "Out catching"—he smirked—"butterflies?"

That should not be a sarcastic question. Lots of people catch butterflies for lots of good, scientific reasons. But from Merrill, the question was an insult, even without the smirk.

"No butterflies," Burton said mildly. He would be nice to Merrill—no matter how hard, he would be nice. Even if Merrill didn't especially know how to be nice himself.

His forehead puckered, Merrill tried to figure out what was going on here. "Holding it up like that is slowing you down, you know."

"Right," said Burton. Even at this distance, he could hear the merriment of the little kids in the playlot.

"But why?" probed Merrill, riding backward, his eyes shifting from Burton's face to the wind sock and back again. "Huh?"

Burton hated to be picked at. Niceness went just so far. "Science," he said shortly. "An experiment." He put on speed, heading toward the sounds of happy kids.

Kevin had stopped fooling around when Merrill turned up. Now he rolled smoothly at Burton's side, there if Burton needed him.

Jonathan dropped back slightly, watching Burton carefully, keeping an eye on Merrill as he showed off some of his fancy tricks on the walk in front of them. If Merrill was up to something, he, Jonathan, was going to find out what it was.

Laughter lifted around them, floating in the air, as they neared the playlot. Burton rolled around the edges, well back from the seesaws and sandbox. He wouldn't go too near—that might be dangerous for the little kids. But even at the outer edges of the playlot, the sounds of fun were loud—squeals and shrieks and giggles.

Burton looked up at the wind sock. It was filled with air and—he hoped—risible ions. He couldn't help smiling. Who wouldn't smile with all that good feeling in the air?

Hey! Another idea! Get a tape of all that laughter. It could be catching. He stowed the idea away in a corner of his brain somewhere above his left ear. He would work on it later.

After a time, grown-ups began to gather up children to take them home at the end of the afternoon. Suddenly, sounds of misery began to creep into the laughter. Wails of protest. Loud *No*'s.

Hastily, Burton lowered the wind sock. He didn't raise it again until they neared the entrance to the park.

Jonathan noticed how Merrill watched Burton with his ferretlike eyes, never taking them off Burton's face. Not, that is, until they passed one of the benches. A man sat there, nearly hidden by the paper he was reading. He lowered it as Burton rolled past.

Jonathan recognized him at once. Professor Savvy, it was—the wily professor himself, the very one who had tried to take Burton's va-ROOOM machine. The professor's eyes shifted from Burton to Merrill and back to Burton.

Did Merrill's eyes, just for an instant, leave Burton's face and look directly into Professor Savvy's eyes? The professor lifted his newspaper and disappeared behind it.

Was something going on between Professor Savvy and Frobusher? But how could that be? The professor was really smart. You had to admit that, even if you didn't approve of him. It didn't take a great brain to see that Merrill was, to put it kindly, the very opposite of smart. So, what could those two possibly have in common? If they did. If their eyes actually had met.

It had all happened in an instant as they rolled past the benches.

Now Jonathan really did have something to think about.

11 _____

Suspicions

*M*errill dropped away when they came out of the park onto Aspidistra Drive. "Got things to do," he yelled over his shoulder, heading off down the street.

Jonathan stood looking after him, undecided. Should he follow Merrill to see whether he would cut back into the park and talk to the professor? Or should he keep an eye on Burton?

Merrill whizzed on past the east entrance to the park. So whatever the "things" were that he had to do, they did not involve the professor.

Stay with Burton, Jonathan decided.

He put on speed to catch up, still thinking. Should he tell Burt about his suspicions? Or leave him in peace to finish his new invention? Better say something, he decided, as he caught up with him. It just might be important.

"Listen, Burt," he said as they turned the corner into Petunia Street. "I saw Professor Savvy just now. He was sitting in the park. Do you suppose he's up to something?"

"How could he be?" Burton asked mildly. "He didn't know we were coming to the park."

True. Jonathan himself hadn't known until Burt led the way with his purple-socked tennis racket.

"Yeah, you're probably right," said Jonathan. His imagination was carrying him away. Just because there had been a problem with weird Professor Savvy once didn't mean there would be a problem with him again.

When they rolled into the driveway Little Brother was still in the backyard, sitting on the back steps, his baseball cap lying beside him.

Tish was still swinging, stretching her toes into the air and pumping to keep herself going.

Clinton and Punker were chasing each other around the yard. Every time Punker went near the gate into the alley, Clinton cut him off and steered him back

into the middle of the yard. That Clinton! Did he think he was a sheepdog looking after a stray lamb?

Burton's hands were full—he was holding the purple wind sock tight at the top to keep the laugh ions from escaping. Little Brother got up from the steps to open the workshop door for him. He held it wide and Burton disappeared inside.

Little Brother gave a whistle. "Come on, Clint," he called.

Clinton hung back, looking from Little Brother to his new little pal, Punker.

"Clint, come on," Little Brother ordered, his voice firm.

With a look of long-suffering patience, Clinton dragged himself into the workshop and Little Brother closed the door. He was not being rude to Burton's friends. They all understood that Burton had important work to do in there.

Tish jumped off the swing in midair, landing on her toes, skipping. "Got to be getting home," she said. "Ready, Punker?"

Punker was on the back steps. He had found Little Brother's baseball cap lying there and had settled down with it, his sharp baby teeth sunk into the bill.

"Punker, don't you dare!" yelled Tish, rushing to the steps. She dropped to her knees, her eyes level with Punker's, and shook a finger in his face. "If you chew on that cap, so help me I'm going to take you out to the country myself and leave you there and never, never, come to see you."

Punker lifted his large, baby eyes to hers. Slowly he relaxed his jaws. The cap dropped.

"That's better," said Tish. "Good dog. Good puppy."

Punker's tail waved.

Tish gathered him up.

"Hey, maybe you're beginning to get through to him," said Kevin.

"I'd better," sighed Tish. Worry lines appeared between her brows. "I don't have long to do it. My mom is getting really uptight."

Tish's troubles reminded Kevin of his own. "Kids' traffic court is Saturday morning," he said. "I wonder if I'll get grounded," he worried.

Kevin's and Tish's troubles brought Jonathan back into his. "How can I stay in the spy business without my stuff?" he moaned. "I sure don't know how I can get it back from the Big Ds." The Big Ds—that had become his name for Miss Doyle and Mr. Dedmun.

"Hey," said Kevin. "I just thought of something. Did you ever notice how much 'Dedmun' sounds like 'dead man'?"

Jonathan didn't need to be reminded. He shuddered.

The miseries had returned. Gloomily they headed for home.

Inside the workshop, Burton had rigged up another jug. He had cut off the toe of the purple sock and it dangled inside the jug. He trained Mama's hair dryer into the top of the sock, blowing into it, transferring all the happy-little-kid ions from the sock into the jug.

"If this doesn't have happy ions," he said to Little Brother, "nothing will." Suddenly he remembered the idea that had come to him in the park. "Do you think," he asked, "you could tape some people laughing?"

Little Brother didn't know what Burton was getting at. "Like tape it off the TV?" he asked.

Burton shook his head. "No. I need the real thing.

You've got to tape right where the laughing people are."

"Like at a movie?" asked Little Brother. "There's a funny one over at Cinema Two. Only I haven't got enough money to get in."

Burton shook his head. "There's lots of free laughing. All you've got to do is look for it. I found some in the park just now."

"Well, sure. I can do that." Little Brother was always agreeable. "Is it something else for the nudger?"

Burton explained. "Just hearing happy sounds makes you feel good."

Little Brother caught the idea. "Someone in the giggle machine will get to feeling better just hearing all kinds of happy people."

"That's the idea," said Burton.

"I'll do it after school tomorrow," promised Little Brother.

12

Misery Loves Company

*J*ust because things are bad doesn't mean they can't get worse. As a matter of fact, the First Law of Misery is "What's bad will get worse." The Second Law of Misery is "Bad things happen in threes." The Third Law is "Misery loves company."

Tish and Kevin and Jonathan proved the Third Law. They put their heads together every day and talked about their troubles. This particular morning they were standing inside the school yard, behind the row of tall bushes that separated the playground from the walk that led to the front door.

"Punker chewed up a corner of the hall carpet," Tish reported. "My mom put in a call to the farm and asked Aunt Ellie when she and Uncle Em are coming to town. They said next week. My mom said to stop in." Tish thought she knew what that meant.

"I wonder if Mr. Dedmun is making stuff with my chemistry set," said Jonathan. "And I wonder if Miss Doyle is practicing to be a superspy."

Kevin's troubles got worse as they stood there. He was, as usual, fooling around with his lariat, but he was talking about kids' traffic court. "I don't know whether I wish Saturday would hurry up and get here so I can get it over with," he said, "or I wish it could be put off—but then I'd only keep on worrying." He spun the lariat overhead and tossed it at the tall bush beside Tish. "Gotcha!" he said, pleased with himself, as the loop landed neatly over the bush.

"Got who!" thundered a deep voice.

The rope jerked out of Kevin's hands.

Mr. Dedmun appeared from the walk behind the bush, untangling himself from the lariat, lifting it off the bush. "Come with me, young man," he said, crooking a finger at Kevin.

Kevin turned white and followed Mr. Dedmun into the building.

"Ohhhh," sighed Tish, watching him go.

"Poor guy," muttered Jonathan. "I know what he's in for."

Later, after the bell rang, Kevin was missing from class. He came into the room in the middle of spelling review. He was still pale, and he was without his lariat.

That's when Burton knew. Ready or not, he had to start using the giggle machine to help his friends. He was going to challenge the First Law of Misery, that what is bad will get worse. Maybe if he helped his friends feel better, they would begin to find answers to their problems. But first he had to get through the school day.

"You may ask questions," Miss Doyle boomed during class project time as everybody bent and carved and shaped their cardboard pieces.

Tish had a question. "Is it a snail?" she asked.

"Tell us why you think it might be a snail," boomed Miss Doyle.

Tish had been giving the class project a lot of thought. "Well"—she spoke slowly—"a snail is an animal. And it carries its shell around with it. And its shell is made of something hard, maybe minerals." That Tish! She was really some thinker!

"Rather good thinking is going on here," said Miss Doyle.

Everybody looked proud of Tish.

"But we are not constructing a snail," said Miss Doyle.

Everybody groaned.

"Burton?" boomed Miss Doyle. "You have been too quiet lately. What are you thinking?"

Actually, Burton had been thinking about the invention. But he certainly could not say that. For a change, though, he knew what was going on in the room. And he had been thinking about the class project, too. He had a question. "When you said what we're making is animal *and* mineral, did you mean its bones? Because bones are minerals."

Miss Doyle was thoughtful. "Yes," she said at last, "bones. Bones are indeed minerals."

Burton was puzzled. "But then it can be anything that's alive. Because all animals have bones."

Kevin picked up on that. "Flies are alive, and they haven't got bones. Spiders, either."

"True," said Miss Doyle. "Nevertheless, I suggest you think *bones*. And minerals."

And that's all she would say.

A sigh swept through the room. Why didn't Miss Doyle teach the way other teachers did—straight facts. Why was she always making them *think*!

Jonathan's spy instincts had started working. There were clues here. He was sure of it. Were the kids getting close to the truth with their questions? What did Miss Doyle mean when she said "think bones"?

It was a quiet classroom day. The miseries were never far away. When the last bell rang, the kids stuffed their books into their backpacks and headed for home, considering their troubles as they strolled.

Burton didn't mope with them. He excused himself and jogged on ahead. There was one last thing he wanted to do with the giggle machine.

He went straight to the workshop, passing the kitchen door without a glance. He was wrapped in his thoughts, in what he meant to do. Whipping the sheet off the giggle machine, he stood back and studied it. Overall, it looked sort of like the prow of a ship. But the details were different, of course.

The foot pads, covered with little bumps, were in place. The mirror was mounted at face level. The cap with its earflaps dangled overhead. A tape deck fit onto the shelf at the back, and speakers were mounted above it, left and right.

He dragged a fan from the corner and placed it in front of the machine, where it would blow across the mouth of the ion jug. Should he use some of the precious laugh ions? Maybe not, this time around—they were hard to come by. Getting them took a lot of time. Still, though . . . if this was to be a true test, he had better check them out. No telling what might happen when those ions flew into a person's face. . . . He uncorked the jug.

"Hey! What are you doing?" asked Little Brother, coming into the workshop with Clinton at his heels as usual. He saw the empty workbench. Empty, that is of food. Something was going on here for sure! "Aren't you hungry? Want me to fix something to eat?"

Burton shook his head. He scarcely heard the questions. Food was the last thing on his mind. "You never saw such sad kids," he said. "I've got to get this ready to use now. Right now."

Little Brother's eyes widened. "But you haven't tested it," he protested. "You can't just use it on people without testing it! If it doesn't work the way you think it will . . . I mean, what if there's an accident and somebody gets hurt? I mean, you don't really know what will happen."

"That's right," said Burton. "So I'm going to test it. Right now. On me."

13

The Big Test

*L*ittle Brother thought about that for a moment. "But you can't watch yourself being tested and see if everything's okay," he said. "Why not test it on me? Then you'll be able to watch what happens."

Burton shook his head. "No way." He couldn't let Little Brother be a guinea pig. If the giggle machine wasn't safe . . . "It's up to me to do this," he said firmly. "But you can help. See this button?" He fingered a button on the control panel. It was marked PB. "It's a panic button. You push it if something weird happens."

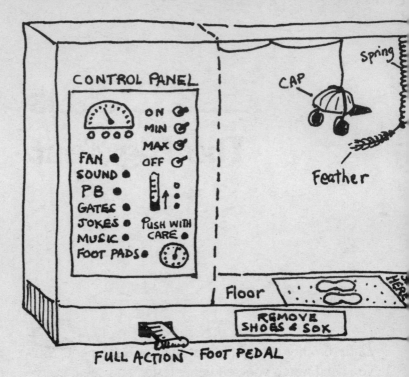

CONTROL PANEL

ON
MIN
MAX
OFF

FAN
SOUND
PB
GATES
JOKES
MUSIC
FOOT PADS

PUSH WITH
CARE

Spring

CAP

Feather

Floor

HERE

REMOVE
SHOES & SOX

FULL ACTION FOOT PEDAL

"What weird?" asked Little Brother.

Burton shrugged. He didn't know. That's why he had to test the invention. "Just keep your eyes on me. Like if I start to cry instead of laughing, push it. It will shut everything down. Only I don't think anything weird will happen."

He showed Little Brother the rest of the buttons and knobs and switches and explained what each one did.

CUTAWAY VIEW INSIDE GIGGLE MACHINE

Mirror

Window

fan

Bubble Cup

Cork

IONS

Fresh Kum Quats

FRESH KIWIS

Little Brother listened carefully, asking an occasional question. "What does *Max* mean?"

"Maximum action," said Burton. "*Min* means minimum action. It's probably best to start slow and work up to high."

"I've got it," Little Brother said after a while, and stationed himself at the ready. He was in charge, and that made him feel grown up and good.

Burton took off his shoes and socks. He mounted

the footpads, fitted the cap with its earflaps onto his head, and adjusted the mirror. "Ready?" he asked Little Brother. "We'll test one thing at a time before we go to full action."

"Ready."

"Fan," said Burton.

"Fan." Little Brother touched a button. The fan whirred into life, blowing across the open mouth of the ion jug, straight at Burton's face. It blew as well through a ring that dipped in and out of a cup of soapy water. Soap bubbles floated around Burton's head.

"Sound," said Burton.

"Sound." Little Brother flipped a switch.

Laughter from one of the tapes blasted from the speakers, bouncing off the walls, rattling the windows.

From his place beside the invention safe, Clinton leaped straight up in the air, yelping.

Outside in the alley, two figures jumped back from the wall against which their ears had been pressed.

"Hey! What's goin' on in there?" yelped Merrill Frobusher.

"Curiosity, curiosity, calm thyself," murmured the professor, speaking to himself.

Fortunately, the skulkers did not have X-ray eyes. They could not look through the wall and into the workshop.

Inside, Burton shouted, "Softer!", his voice drowned out by the uproar.

"Softer," said Little Brother, reading Burton's lips. He spun a knob. The roar softened until only the good sound of chuckles and giggles swirled around the invention. "Jokes?" he asked.

"Okay, jokes," Burton agreed.

"Hear this," a voice intoned in Burton's right ear. Burton listened. "That's a good one," he chuckled, slapping his knee. "Now music."

"Music," said Little Brother. A jig sounded from the speakers.

"Lever," ordered Burton.

"Lever," repeated Little Brother, stepping on the full-action foot pedal.

The invention rumbled. The fan picked up speed, sending a flood of laugh ions into Burton's face and a flurry of bubbles in and around the giggle machine. The laugh track skipped to the good part where people were chortling with glee. A second joke tape activated, feeding jokes into Burton's left ear. He was getting jokes now in both ears. The jig quickened its foot-tapping rhythm. And the bumps on the foot pads began to quiver.

"Yikes!" Burton laughed, hopping straight up. At the top of his hop, a feather tickled his nose. "Yeeks!" He laughed, sneezing, landing back on the rippling foot pads.

Up and down he went, from one tickle to the next. Up, tickle, down, tickle, all of it happening to the lilt of the jig. With each hop he glimpsed himself in the mirror, his face bending and bulging.

Burton let out a belly laugh, caught his breath, and laughed some more. And he kept on laughing.

Little Brother was watchful, his eyes on Burton in case there was trouble.

Clinton watched, too, his head tilted to one side. After a moment he added to the general hoopla. "Ar-rOOO," he howled. "Ar-rOOOOO."

Laughing as he was, with tears streaming down his face, Burton was not able to tell Little Brother when to stop the test. Little Brother had to use his own judgment.

He eyed the many parts of the invention. He could only guess what jokes Burton was hearing, but the dial showed that both of the joke tapes were in operation. He checked out the fan, the feather, the mirror, the tape recorders. He listened to the jig. He watched Burton hopping up and down, caught in laughter.

Everything seemed to be working just fine.

"Cut," he said, and flipped the Off switch. The giggle machine ground down into silence.

Burton stepped off the foot pads and leaned against the machine, gasping and hiccuping. He mopped at his eyes.

"I guess the invention passed the test, huh?" said Little Brother.

"You better believe it," Burton gasped on a last left-over chuckle.

"And I guess it's a success," said Little Brother. "I mean, you sure did laugh."

"I sure did," Burton agreed. But—was the invention a success simply because he had laughed? He thought about that. Then he realized something: The whole time he was in the giggle machine he had not worried about whether it was safe or not, or whether it would really help his friends or not. So maybe it really did do what he had set out to do.

He sat down to pull on his socks and shoes and asked himself a final question. Now that he was out of the machine, did he still feel better?

He tied his shoelaces and stood up. He grinned. Yep. He felt good. He felt great. He felt as though he could meet any challenge and whip it. "Bring on the challenges," he murmured.

"Huh?" asked Little Brother.

"If there's a problem, I know I can handle it," Burton explained.

"And that means if you can do it . . ." Little Brother's voice trailed off.

"—so can Tish and Jonathan and Kevin," said Burton. "Tomorrow," he said, "after school, we go into action."

That evening, the Knockwursts were seen making their usual trip to the workshop.

"The girl is carrying something," hissed Merrill Frobusher, crouched behind a bush in a neighboring yard.

"The father has a large envelope," muttered Professor Savvy, kneeling beside him. "Now keep your eyes open. See how things are when they leave."

Moments later, the family returned to the house. Little Brother fastened the workshop's big padlock and followed them.

"The girl and the father aren't carrying anything," whispered Merrill.

"Good lad! You have sharp eyes," said the professor.

"Well, sure," said Merrill. "I'm better than most at seeing things." Then, "What do you suppose it all means?" he asked.

"Where there are questions, there are answers." The professor sounded very wise. "We are going to find those answers."

One by one, as the evening wore on, the lights in the house went out. First in the children's rooms upstairs, then downstairs in the living room, and at last in the grown-ups' bedroom.

The night was moonless, starless, windless. It wore on.

In the deep dark before dawn, two figures approached the workshop. One of them reached for the lock on the door.

The noise was whisper-soft. But Clinton heard it. A chorus of barking erupted in the night.

Little Brother leaped out of bed, still half-asleep, grabbed his flashlight, and dashed downstairs barefoot. He got as far as the kitchen door, where Clinton was jumping and barking wildly, before a hand on his shoulder brought him to a stop.

"Why, Little Brother!" said Mama. "You are walking in your sleep. Come back to bed, lovey."

"I'm not walking in my sleep," protested Little Brother. "I'm—"

"There now," Mama said soothingly. "You've had a bad dream."

"There's somebody outside," insisted Little Brother. "I want to know who it is."

"Yes, yes," Mama cooed, drawing him away from the door.

"Listen to Clinton," said Little Brother. "Just listen to the noise he's making."

Mama listened. But Clinton had quieted abruptly. The skulkers were gone, frightened away by his barking army. He settled down at the door.

"See?" Mama said softly. "You were dreaming, my pet—just dreaming. Now come back to bed and Mama will sing to you."

Miserably, Little Brother let himself be led upstairs and tucked in. Well, he could be led to bed, but he couldn't be made to sleep. So there!

Mama sang gentle songs, "Love's Old Sweet Song" and "Ramona."

As soon as Mama stopped singing, Little Brother told himself, he was going to . . . he was going to . . . His eyelids opened . . . closed . . . opened . . . closed—and stayed closed.

Mama leaned over and kissed him. She tucked the blankets around his shoulders and tiptoed back to her own room. How lucky that she had heard Little Brother and stopped him from sleepwalking away from his bad dream!

14

Giggle Machine at Work

"*Y*ou're gonna let us see your new invention!" Kevin exclaimed when, on the way home from school, Burton announced he wanted them all to stop at the workshop. "What is it?"

"Well," said Burton, "it's something that might—uh—help you guys fix your problems."

"Punker's chewing," breathed Tish. "You found a way to cure him!"

"No kids' traffic court!" Kevin exulted. "You got me out of it!"

"You're gonna get my book and my chemistry set back from the Big Ds!" exclaimed Jonathan.

"Wait-wait-wait!" said Burton. "Not me. I can't do those things. *You* can. But maybe I can give you a lift." And that's all he would say.

As they passed Tish's house, she begged, "Wait, oh, wait for me. I've got to pick up Punker." She dashed into the house and came back cuddling the puppy. "I don't leave him alone any more than I have to," she explained. "He gets into terrible trouble when he's by himself."

They trooped on to the Knockwursts'. Little Brother was already there. He had gotten home from school early, had checked the mailbox—nothing was there—had fixed himself a snack, and was waiting for them in front of the workshop. No way was he going to miss this first real trial of the giggle machine.

Everybody crowded around Burton, eager to follow him inside.

He came to a standstill, confused. He hadn't thought about this, about the kids watching each other in the giggle machine. Maybe that wasn't a good idea. Maybe being surprised was part of what would make it work to maximum effect. . . . Of course . . . he hadn't been surprised himself, and the machine worked for him. . . . Still, though . . .

"Burt?" Tish snapped her fingers in front of his face.

"You're thinking again, Burt."

"Yeah. Don't get lost on us," said Jonathan.

"Come on, Burt," pleaded Kevin. "Don't make us wait."

Burton made up his mind. "You can't all come in at once," he told them. "You'll have to come in one at a time."

Nobody liked that idea at all.

"Me first!"

"No, me!"

"Hey! Who wants to be last!"

Little Brother listened. While everybody argued, he bent, pulled three blades of grass, and held them between his palms. He offered his hands. "Pick a straw. Short one goes first, longest straw last."

That seemed fair.

Tish drew the short straw. Jonathan drew the longest.

"Jon and I will wait," sighed Kevin, who hated doing things in slow motion. It was his secret wish that Burton would invent a speedup machine—push a button and time would zip forward so that nobody ever had to wait for anything. But Burton hadn't done that yet. "We'll wait," he said again, and sat down, leaning against the workshop wall, surrounded by pink and purple petunias. Jonathan joined him.

Tish followed Burton into the workshop and set

Punker down inside the door. Clinton came running from the side yard and slid through the opening just as Little Brother closed the door.

Burton whipped the sheet off the giggle machine and tossed it aside.

Punker skittered across the room and tugged at a corner of the sheet.

Clinton trotted after him and nudged him away.

Tish inspected the impressive-looking machine. It was pretty overwhelming. As a matter of fact, it was kind of scary. "Am I supposed to get into that?" she asked warily. "It looks kind of like it might chop me up."

"It won't," Burton reassured her. "I tested it yesterday on me. And look at me—I'm all in one piece. And I feel great," he added.

"But what's it going to do?" Tish asked. "I mean, I trust you, Burt, but—"

"You're going to laugh a lot," said Burton, and while she took off her shoes and socks he went on to talk about some of the things that were going to happen. "Maybe you'll feel good when you get out of the machine," he finished. "And maybe you'll be able to figure out how to get Punker out of trouble."

Tish's face softened. "There isn't anything I wouldn't do for Punker," she said softly. "Listen! If you give me a lift, maybe he will catch it. You know—like catching mumps. And if he gets a lift, maybe he'll stop his, his"—she made a face, searching for the worst word she knew—"*glonky* chewing."

"Yip," barked Punker from his place at Clinton's side.

"Okay," said Tish, putting on the cap. "I'm ready."

"Let's go," said Burton. He stepped on the full-action pedal.

The giggle machine churned into life.

The cool current of the fan stirred Tish's bangs. She lifted her face to the cooling breeze—and to the laugh ions it carried. Bubbles floated around her head, glinting in the light.

Laughter filled the room and the corners of her mouth tipped upward.

She tittered at the first joke and did a few steps of a clog dance when the jig began—or it would have been a clacking clog routine if she had been wearing shoes. But then there was no more dancing as the foot pads went into action.

Burton folded his arms and watched, chuckling, remembering his own experiences of yesterday. Little Brother laughed along with him. Clinton added his "ar-roooo" to the fun. Punker ran in circles around the giggle machine, yipping.

Then Punker lost interest. Tish's shoes and socks were temptingly close. He picked up a sock.

Clinton made him put it down and hustled him back to their place beside the invention safe.

The giggle machine acted for Tish exactly as it had for Burton. When it whirred to a stop, she went on laughing, her cheeks pink, her eyes dancing.

"What a great," she gasped, "absolutely stu-stupendous invention!"

Punker came running. "Oh, Punkie," she said, picking him up, hugging him, "you've just got to turn into a good, responsible puppy. You've just got to."

Punker licked her chin.

Outside, Jonathan and Kevin had listened to the ruckus, exchanging wondering glances. What in heck was going on in the workshop?

Kevin found out next, when he took his turn in the giggle machine. And in time, Jonathan found out, too.

On the far side of Petunia Street, the skulkers peeked out from behind a bush.

"They go into the workshop one at a time," said Merrill. "You have to wonder why they don't all go in at once. I mean, they're friends."

Later, as everybody came out together, the professor muttered, "Why do they all look so dratted happy? What can be going on in there? My curiosity is approaching the boiling point. I don't know how much longer I can keep the lid on it."

15

Kids' Traffic Court

Well, of course they couldn't let Kevin go to kids' traffic court all by himself! And so the next morning he found Burton and the others waiting for him when he came out of his house, his face shining clean, his hair slicked down with water, and wearing his second-best pair of sneakers because they were whiter than his very best pair.

"You okay, Kev?" asked Burton.

"Uh-huh," said Kevin. "You know, I laughed so hard yesterday that I felt good right up to bedtime last night.

And I've thought how I'm gonna answer whatever that judge asks me. I'm gonna be okay."

"You're really gonna be okay," they all chorused.

Kevin grinned. He had the look about him of someone who can handle any challenge. He practiced his polite yes-ma'ams and no-sirs and give-you-my-words all the way to city hall. Actually, he sort of chattered. But nobody interrupted him. It was better for him to chatter than to be glum and gloomy.

At city hall, they followed him up the broad stone steps and across the wide plaza. Jonathan pointed at a row of first-floor windows. "That's the room," he said, "right inside the door. I checked it out the other day."

Suddenly a security guard appeared out of nowhere. "Whoa, there, you kids," he called. "No dogs allowed in city hall."

Tish got her stubborn look. "If Punker isn't welcome, neither am I," she sniffed. "We'll wait out here."

"Me, too," said Little Brother. "Sit, Clinton. Sit."

Clinton sat.

Burton hung back. "I guess we'll all wait out here, Kev," he said.

"But if you really need us," Jonathan muttered in a low voice the security guard could not pick up, "give a whistle and we'll storm the place."

"Gotcha," said Kevin. He threw back his shoulders,

marched to the heavy glass doors, and paused, looking back at them. "Challenge, here I come," he said. He looked firm and sure of himself.

They gave him the thumbs-up sign and the door closed behind him.

The security guard stationed himself beside the door, folded his arms, and looked as though he meant to keep dogs out if they tried to get in.

A low wall enclosed the plaza. They settled on it to wait.

Kevin appeared for a moment in a window off to the right and waved at them. They waved back. Then a grown-up touched Kevin's shoulder and he disappeared.

Punker scampered around the plaza playing while they waited. Idly they watched. Punker made for the glass doors. Clinton cut him off and edged him back toward Tish.

Someone had dropped a rolled-up newspaper nearby. Punker headed for it. He got a good mouthful before Clinton made him drop it.

"Here, boy," called Tish, digging around in her jacket pocket. She brought out a rubber chewbone. "Play with this, Punkie," she said, offering it on her outstretched hand.

Punker took it and began to chew.

Clinton watched him. Most of the time he let him chomp away on the toy. But sometimes he stopped him just to show who was boss. He picked up the bone and dropped it at a distance. When Punker went near it, Clinton got in the way and made him wait. Punker sat, his eyes bright, watching Clinton, waiting for permission.

"I had a good dream last night," said Tish. "I dreamed that Punker sat up and told me—he could talk in this dream—that he wasn't going to chew down our house."

"Last night while I was loading the dishwasher," said Jonathan, "my mom asked me what I was smiling about. I didn't know I was smiling. I was thinking about the giggle machine."

Burton listened, thinking. Would Tish and Jonathan be able to solve their problems? Who could say! But they certainly did seem lots happier than they had been yesterday, or any day in the past week.

How long is an eon? That's how long they had to wait for Kevin—or at least for half an hour. But at last the glass doors swung open and he came out onto the plaza. His hair wasn't slicked down anymore, because the water had dried and his curls had popped up. But he looked okay anyway. He was grinning.

"Was the judge mean?" asked Tish. "Did he ground you?"

"Didn't ground me," said Kevin. "And the judge wasn't a he. The judge was a she."

"Well, what did she say you've got to do?" demanded Jonathan.

"She didn't say I've got to do anything," said Kevin. "*I* said what I've got to do."

They stared at him.

"Well, see," he went on, "the judge said I'd been riding my skateboard way too fast for public safety and then she said, 'What am I going to do with you?' and I said, 'I guess you've got to tell me not to ride so fast anymore,' and she said, 'Very good. And what else?' and I said, 'I guess I've got to promise.' So then she said, 'And do you promise?' and I said, 'Oh, yes, ma'am!' "

He took a deep breath. "Then she asked me what a promise was. I said, 'It's giving your word about something and you've got to keep your word even if someone says they'll give you a billion dollars to break the promise.' Then she said, 'Can you think of anything that might help you keep your promise not to endanger the public safety?' So I said, 'I guess I could use a speedometer,' and she said, 'Very good. Now I don't want to see you in this court ever again.' I said, 'No, ma'am!' and she said, 'You may go.' "

He let out a long breath after that long speech. He was feeling lots better than he had felt for days and days.

Then he remembered. "Burt," he asked, "can you invent a speedometer for me so I won't endanger the public safety anymore?"

Burton didn't see any problem with that request. After the va-ROOOM machine and the giggle machine, inventing a speedometer would be a snap. "I'll put a whistle on it," he said. "When you hit top speed, the whistle will blow and you'll know it's slow-down time."

104

Everybody looked cheerful. After all Kevin's worrying, kids' traffic court had not been too terrible.

They still had the whole day ahead of them. Everybody had Saturday things to do. It was time to be getting on home.

Little Brother wanted to get back to the workshop to check out the lock on the door. And he had to check out the mailbox, too.

Tish had to go home. She was going to work with Punker. She was going to take him around the house to everything he had chewed and show things to him and shake her finger and say no in a loud voice. No, *no, no!*

Jonathan had to go to the library. "There's something I've got to look up," he said. "I've got sort of an idea about the class project."

They all wanted to know what it was, but he wouldn't say. He just headed off down the street, jogging.

Burton had to get back to the workshop, too. He had to put together Kevin's speedometer.

And so they went their separate ways. The security guard stood watching them go. He didn't unfold his arms and relax until all those dogs—both of them— were clear away from city hall.

16

Superspy in Action

"You said you have questions to ask, Jonathan," harrumphed Miss Doyle. "You may begin."

It was Monday. They were back in school.

Burton had spent the weekend in the workshop. Kevin's speedometer was finished, except for the whistle.

Kevin had spent the weekend practicing going slow on his skateboard. It wasn't nearly as much fun as going fast, but he had a promise to keep.

Tish had spent the weekend saying no, *no, no!* to

Punker and taking him to Burton's house to be near Clinton. Clinton did not chew on things. Clinton might be a good influence on Punker.

Jonathan had spent all his free time at the library hunting up information and then using his superspy skills to add up the facts in interesting ways. He had come to school today with a list of questions for Miss Doyle.

"You said we'd find clues about the class project in your answers to our questions, and we should add them up," he said. "And you said what we're making is an animal and a mineral. And it's not a snail, like Tish thought. Right?"

"Correct," said Miss Doyle. "On all points, correct."

"And you said"—Jonathan checked his list—"to think bones and minerals. Bones are minerals—I checked that out at the library. Well, are the bones always made of the same minerals? Or do they change?"

Miss Doyle's left eyebrow lifted. Was that a spark of interest in her eyes? She frowned. No. It could not have been a spark of interest. She had a question for Jonathan. "Will you explain yourself further? I am not sure I understand."

Eyes in the room went from Miss Doyle to Jonathan. Something interesting was going on here!

"The minerals in the bones," said Jonathan carefully, "are they the same when the animal is alive as when it's dead?"

There was a spark in Miss Doyle's eyes! It was not wiped out by a frown! "I rather think," she said, "that they are not."

Good! He was getting somewhere! Jonathan was sure of it. He went to another point on his list. "When Burton asked if the animal lives in North America, you didn't say yes or no. It was kind of funny the way you said, 'You will *find* it on this continent.' So maybe you were telling us it doesn't live here now, but it used to live here. And we know about animals that lived a long time ago because we find their bones. So, are those the bones you meant we should think about?"

"Now isn't this fun!" boomed Miss Doyle, looking around at everybody brightly.

Feet shuffled. Breaths were let out. Jonathan, superspy-to-be, was finding the answers to Miss Doyle's challenge.

"But," she went on, "what does finding bones have to do with minerals that are the same or different in those bones?"

A warm glow began to fill Jonathan. But he was careful not to let it get in the way of his thinking. "Well, see," he said, "I read in a book that when dinosaurs died, they got covered up with mud and stuff, and water ran over their bones and put minerals in them, and the bones turned into fossils. Fossils are stones, and stones are minerals. So, dinosaurs used to be alive and then they died and their bones turned into stone minerals. What we're building: I betcha it's a dinosaur."

The room was still. All faces turned to Miss Doyle.

And then—and then—Miss Doyle laughed. She did. She let out a big, booming laugh. "You are thinking, boy. I hope you are enjoying it."

Enjoying? Strange—Jonathan had been so busy he had not thought about enjoying. But yeah—this was, in a weird way, fun.

"We," boomed Miss Doyle, looking around at the class, "are constructing a creature of the dinosaur era." Her eyes went back to Jonathan. "Would you care to take a guess at which one?"

Jonathan had not spent two whole days in the library for nothing. "Did the animal live in North America, then, like Burton asked?"

"It did," said Miss Doyle.

He had it! He was sure of it! "Kevin said the slabs he's making look like the tiles on his roof. I read in one of the books about a North American dinosaur called a 'roofed lizard' because it had bony things on its back that the guy who found it thought looked like shingles on a roof. Its fancy name was Stegosaurus. Are we making a Stegosaurus?"

Miss Doyle let out a big sigh. It sounded like a hurricane rushing through the room. "Your deductive powers have stood you in good stead, Jonathan."

The warm glow engulfed Jonathan.

"Which is to say," she continued, "that you have put two and two together and arrived at our answer. We are in truth constructing a Stegosaurus."

A cheer went up from the class.

Jonathan sank back into his seat, grinning. Wow! All that library time had been worth it!

The door opened with a bang. "What is the meaning of this uproar?" thundered Mr. Dedmun.

The room was instantly silent. The plink-plunk of water dripping in the utility sink sounded like someone banging on a drum.

"Well?" he rumbled.

Miss Doyle knew how to handle emergencies like this one. She folded her hands across her middle, drew herself up, and said, "You will be pleased to know that one of our—ahem—researchers—ahem—has supplied us with the name of our class project."

Mr. Dedmun looked grumpy, waiting for her to go on.

Miss Doyle did, looking proud. "Jonathan, stand up."

Jonathan did, uneasily. He did not like having to stand and be looked at by Mr. Dedmun.

Miss Doyle continued. "He did this relying solely on his powers of deduction and library research. He solved the riddle of the class project. Jonathan, would you care to tell Mr. Dedmun the name of the creature?"

Jonathan took a deep breath. "A dinosaur," he squeaked.

"Called a—?" Miss Doyle prompted.

"Stegosaurus," said Jonathan.

Mr. Dedmun looked grumpily impressed.

"Jonathan," Miss Doyle suggested, "I am sure you would like to share your research with Mr. Dedmun. Please tell him about Stegosaurus."

Jonathan blinked, digging around in his mind for facts . . . facts . . . what were some facts? He remembered one. "Twenty feet long," he squeaked. "It was twenty feet long." That fact led to more. His voice got stronger. "It weighed almost two tons, but its brain was only as big as this." He held up a hand, two fingers circled, to show how tiny Stegosaurus's brain was.

Miss Doyle stood there, hands on her middle, looking proud. Yes, she really did look proud. "So you see, Mr. Dedmun, the slight bit of unseemly noise you heard was just a gust of approval for our researcher."

"Well." Mr. Dedmun cleared his throat. "As long as we don't go in for this academic cheering too often, I will let it pass this time." He turned to leave. Then he swung around and looked at Jonathan again, and then at Miss Doyle. "Isn't this the boy who . . . who . . ."

"Yes." Miss Doyle nodded. "And now that you mention it, I believe it's safe to return his chemistry set to him. He is becoming quite responsible."

"Are you responsible, Jonathan?" demanded Mr. Dedmun.

"Yes, sir!" Jonathan hoped he had a responsible look on his face.

"And you won't cause any more trouble with your chemistry set here in school—or anywhere?"

"No, sir!" Jonathan drew himself up tall, looking like a boy who would not dream of causing trouble with his chemistry set.

"Hmm," said Mr. Dedmun. "Hmm." His glance roved the room. He seemed to be thinking. Suddenly his eyes came to rest on Kevin.

Kevin shrank down in his seat.

Mr. Dedmun's eyes narrowed. "And you. Do you have anything to say about responsibility?"

Kevin gulped. "It's a good thing," he said.

"Tell me some more," said Mr. Dedmun. "I am very interested in responsibility this morning."

"We all should have some," said Kevin.

"More," said Mr. Dedmun.

"We should think what might happen when we do something," said Kevin. He was sweating.

"More." Would nothing satisfy Mr. Dedmun?

Would he keep saying *more* forever?

"We shouldn't hurt anybody," Kevin said desperately, "or—make them uncomfortable by roping them?" There. He was out of ideas. He had nothing more to say about responsibility.

It satisfied Mr. Dedmun. He didn't say *more* again. He turned to Miss Doyle. "Hmm," he said. "Basing my decision on what I have heard here this morning, I will turn over the chemistry set and the rope to you. You will see to it that these boys act responsibly with them from now on."

"Jonathan and Kevin have shown that they know what responsibility is," said Miss Doyle. "They will be responsible in the future, or they will have me to deal with."

"Grrumphhh," said Mr. Dedmun, or something like that. He turned and left.

Miss Doyle closed the door after him.

"Jonathan, Kevin, you will see me about your property after school. Now let's get on with our class project."

Jonathan struck while things were still looking good. "My book? And my magnifying glass? Can I have those back, too?"

"*May* you have them back," roared Miss Doyle. "We will discuss that, too. Now, people, let's get to work on our Stegosaurus."

The Stegosaurus could not be twenty feet long, of course. But it was still pretty big. They assembled it near the learning center's doors where everyone in school could enjoy it. They used tons of staples and tape and glue. Before the day was over, they even painted it. They made it a kind of muddy, spotty green because Burton said if it walked around in the bushes it was probably camouflaged. So muddy green it was.

Meanwhile, as they worked, something was going on in a laboratory on the far side of town.

Professor Savvy huddled over a row of padlocks lined up on his workbench. They were locks of many kinds. He held one of them and delicately slid a piece of wire into it. "Like this," he said. "You twist it and you turn it. Gently . . . gently and then *poof*! it pops open." He held it up triumphantly.

"I heard it," said Merrill. "It clicked."

"We will refine our technique," said the professor. "We must learn to do this so silently that not even we hear it click."

"Will it take us long to learn to do that?" asked Merrill. "Will it, huh? How long do we have to wait before we go in there?"

The professor thrust one of the padlocks into Merrill's hands. "Patience," he muttered impatiently. "I cannot teach you everything I know overnight. Now you try one of the locks."

17

Second-Best Dog

"So Jonathan got his stink-um set and other stuff back, huh?" said Little Brother, sipping his persimmon-squash shake. "And Kevin got his lariat? Wow! They're out of trouble."

"Yep," said Burton. He bit into his onion-nut sandwich. "All they've got to do now is look up about being responsible and write a report about it for Miss Doyle."

Little Brother made a face. "Lots of work."

"But they'll like doing it," said Burton. "Jonathan's going to look up all the responsible superspies in

116

history. Kevin's going to look up everything about re-sponsible cowboys."

They were in the workshop. The school day was over and Burton could get on with his real life, with his inventions. He fingered the whistle he was finishing for Kevin's speedometer. When the rush of air past his skateboard built up to a certain speed, the whistle would squeal. Not bad, he thought. Nothing fancy. He had put the speedometer together out of bits and pieces, and there wasn't much that could go wrong with it. Simple was always best.

He looked over at the giggle machine. Now that was not simple! It stood there in all its wonderfulness, without its covering. He liked looking at it. The design was great. But what was best, it really did work—the kids felt better. Gone were the glooms. With the glooms licked, they had been able to put their heads to work. Jonathan had solved his problems. Kevin had gotten himself out of his troubles. Tish still had a way to go, but somehow things were going to be okay. He didn't know how, but he was sure of it.

His gaze drifted to the va-ROOOM machine in its daytime place on the back wall. Now why had Little Brother made him promise not to use it for a while? "Listen, Newton," he said—Newton was Little Brother's real name—"I don't know why you made me give my word not to go out on the va-ROOOM machine.

117

So why did you? It's a nice day today. I'd really like to take it for a whirl."

"Hang on just a little longer," Little Brother said seriously. "And then if what I think will happen does, I'll tell you all about it."

"But why not tell—"

He was interrupted by a loud thumping on the door. "Come on out, Burt," called Kevin. "Or let us in."

Burton tucked the speedometer whistle into a cubbyhole in the workbench. He still had to mount the whistle on the speedometer and test it. There was no reason why the kids couldn't come in, though. There wasn't anything they couldn't see today.

Little Brother opened the door and they tumbled into the workshop, laughing. Jonathan was wearing one of his best spy disguises—a black mustache and bushy eyebrows. Kevin was carrying his skateboard. His lariat was looped over his shoulder. Tish was holding Punker. She set him down and he ran across the room to say hello to his buddy Clinton.

They all hunkered down on the floor and leaned against the wall. Their eyes were on the giggle machine.

"That sure is one great invention," sighed Jonathan. "You laugh so hard it sort of clears out your brains."

"Yeah," Kevin agreed. "And then you can think."

"I wonder what will happen with Punker," Tish said

dreamily. "I mean, I've showed him everything I can think of about not chewing on things. I'm sort of sure he's going to be okay. But I don't know how that's going to happen."

"What about your aunt and uncle?" asked Burton. "When are they coming from the farm?"

"My mom said Wednesday," said Tish. "I've got until Wednesday."

"A lot can happen in two days," Little Brother said comfortingly.

"Hey! What about that Miss Doyle," said Kevin. "She really stuck up for you to Mr. Dedmun, Jon."

"Just when you think she's against you," said Jonathan, "she turns around and fights for you."

"She got your chemistry set back for you, Jon," said Tish, "and she got your lariat, Kevin. I wish she could help Punker and me," she added wistfully, looking across the workshop at the little dog.

They followed her gaze. Punker was lying quietly beside Clinton, his nose on his paws.

Click! Suddenly things began to add up in Burton's mind. Clinton and Punker! "Hey, Tish," he said. "Look, there. Punker is lying right next to that tablecloth and he isn't pulling on it."

"Or chewing on it," Tish said wonderingly, "or looking like he plans to."

Burton took an eraser from his pencil tray, crushed

it inside a piece of paper, and tossed it. The paper ball landed right in front of Punker.

The puppy's eyes brightened. Did somebody here want to play with him? He sat up, eyeing the paper, his head cocked to one side. But he didn't touch it.

A slow smile lighted Tish's face. Could it be . . . oh, could it be? "Keep talking, everybody," she said softly. "Don't watch him."

She took off her sneakers. They were blue and white striped, brand-new. She dropped them nearby and pretended to pay them no more notice. She tugged off her socks and tossed them in the air. One landed under the window. The other came to rest near the door.

"This is a test," she said. "Let's see what happens."

They talked. About the giggle machine. About the va-ROOOM machine. They chatted about kids' traffic court and the Stegosaurus and how awful it would be to have a twenty-foot-long body and a pea-sized brain. They pretended not to pay any attention to Punker. But they watched him out of the corners of their eyes.

Clinton got up. He wandered over to the shoes, to one sock, then to the other.

Punker followed him.

Clinton sniffed at each interesting thing. Then he ambled back to his place beside the invention safe.

120

Punker sniffed at everything, too. Then he followed Clinton and settled down beside him.

Clinton yawned. Punker yawned.

Clinton closed his eyes. Punker did, too.

Tish glowed. Punker had learned not to chew! She went to him. "Good dog," she said, cuddling him. "Nice Punkie."

Punker wiggled happily and kissed her chin.

Tish looked around at everybody. Her cheeks were pink. "He got the idea at last," she said happily. "He's learned that chewing is something he's not supposed to do. He learned it from me and from Clinton."

Little Brother had watched with pride. Clinton was the best dog!

Tish gave Clinton a happy, rough petting. "You are a good influence on Punker, Clint. You are the second-most-wonderful dog!"

"Hey!" protested Little Brother.

Clinton opened his mouth. "Ar-roooo," he moaned, as though to say, "I'd like to argue with you about *second*-best."

"What do you mean, second-most-wonderful dog!" demanded Little Brother.

"Well, Punker is *the* most wonderful," said Tish. "Aren't you, Punkie?" she asked, holding him up and looking right into his eyes.

"Yiiiii," agreed Punker.

18

Family Fun Time

*T*he inventions were all safely stowed away in the invention safe for the night. Clinton, the In Operation light on his collar glowing, stretched out in front of the fire, his eyes opening and closing as he watched his family. There wasn't a single thing for anybody to worry about.

The living room was at its cheerful evening best. The fire crackled and popped, sending its dancing light around the room. Papa and Mama, in their matching velvet chairs, sat on either side of the fireplace.

Burton and Edisonia and Little Brother sprawled on the soft carpet. It was family fun time.

Mama did math tricks to amuse them. They set up problems for her and she did them in her head while Papa did them on his calculator to see if she was right. "My love," he asked, "how much is twelve thousand five hundred twenty-seven point zero two times seventy-three?" he clicked away, entering the numbers into the calculator.

"Nine hundred fourteen thousand, four hundred seventy-two point four six," said Mama.

Papa held up the calculator so everybody could see the display.

"She's right," Edisonia said proudly.

"Of course she's right," said Papa. "Children, your mama has an amazing mind. She is never wrong."

"It's really neat not to have to use a calculator," said Burton.

"Oh, I use one sometimes," Mama said modestly. "When I do the really hard numbers. For the think tank, you know."

Next Papa played a tape of his new symphony and showed them how he had conducted it with the Kirksville Philharmonic Orchestra. He kept time with his baton, and he pointed at where violins would have been when it was their turn to play, and he hushed the horns with his other hand when he meant them to play softly. Anyone would have believed there was an orchestra right there in the living room. Papa's baton technique was wonderful to behold.

Edisonia clapped and called for an encore when he finished, but he did not have another tape.

Edisonia couldn't play anything on her invention because the flute of the harp-flute was in the invention safe out in the workshop. But she tap-danced and sang "My Wild Irish Rose." She curtsied deeply when she finished.

"Now here is one for Little Brother," said Papa. He held up a book. "I picked up this book at The Book Shop today, and I know Little Brother has not seen it. Have you, Son?"

Little Brother shook his head. It was a thick book of poems.

"Now," said Papa, "I am opening the book to a page, any page. And I ask Little Brother to read a poem, once, just once."

Little Brother did, while they all watched him, holding their breaths. Even Clinton held his breath.

Little Brother handed the book back to Papa.

Papa smiled. "Tell us," he said. "Say the poem."

Little Brother did. He recited all of "The Shooting of Dan McGrew" while Papa followed, his finger on the page, his lips moving silently. Little Brother didn't miss a single word.

124

Papa looked up, smiling, and led the applause.

Little Brother smiled shyly. He liked knowing his family was proud of him, even though he had never invented anything.

At last it was Burton's turn. He had a surprise for them.

He led the way to the dining room and emptied a box of jigsaw puzzle pieces on the table. He looked around. "Bet you can't finish this before bedtime," he said.

"But it's much too late to start a puzzle," said Mama. "We can't possibly finish it tonight."

"We must be practical," said Papa. "Remember the last puzzle? It was on the table for three days and we had to eat on trays."

Burton grinned. "Trust me," he said. "You won't go to bed wondering what this one is. And we won't have to eat on trays tomorrow."

Little Brother studied Burton's face. Burton was up to something. He was sure of it. "We'd better trust Burton," he said, and found two corner pieces to start the puzzle.

They worked for ages, or so it seemed. Everybody was quiet as they hunted for pieces of sky and buildings and smoke. Edisonia was sure there was smoke in the puzzle.

Clinton trotted around the table, stopping at each

of his people to have his ears scratched. Then he took himself off and lay down in his cozy basket.

At last Mama looked up at the clock. "Bedtime," she said. "Oh, how sorry I am that we can't finish this. Look. I've put together part of an old-time fire engine— I think."

Burton laughed. "Okay, everyone. Watch this."

He pulled a pair of gloves, ordinary work gloves, out of his pocket. At least, they looked ordinary. He put them on. "Ready?" he asked. "Set. Go!"

He moved his hands above the pieces in lazy circles. Slowly the pieces began to move around, to slide into place. Faster . . . faster . . . until finally *zip, slip, flip!* The pieces locked together and there it was, a scene from the Great Chicago Fire of 1871. The puzzle was finished.

"Wonderful!" gasped Mama.

"Amazing," breathed Papa.

"So that's why you've had a puzzle on your workbench," said Little Brother. "I've been wondering about that. It's a new invention. What are you going to do with it?"

"Nothing," said Burton. "Half the fun of jigsaw puzzles is putting them together. It wouldn't be any fun to have it done for you. Nobody will want this invention."

"I bet I know why you invented it, though," said Edisonia.

126

Everybody looked at her, waiting.

"You did it just to see if you could," she said. "Am I right?" Her eyes danced.

"Yep," said Burton. "I've been fooling around with it for a while now, just for the fun of it." He yawned and stretched. "Now I don't ever have to wonder again if it's something I can do."

Then they all had a bedtime snack of honey-corn whip and crackers, and everybody kissed Mama and Papa good-night and gave Clinton a good petting, and they went upstairs to their rooms.

Burton stretched out in bed, his hands under his head, and smiled in the darkness, thinking of the giggle machine. The wonderful giggle machine. . . .

Little Brother curled up, hugging his pillow. He liked hugging something when he went to sleep. He was too big, of course, to hug a stuffed animal. But his pillow was nice.

Edisonia snuggled under her flower-sprigged coverlet and hummed softly to herself. Music always made her happy. She hummed herself to sleep every night.

Night settled around the Knockwurst house, an unusually dark night. No moon shone. No wind stirred the leaves of the butternut tree.

In time, the shuddering cry of an owl quivered in the darkness.

After a moment, the delicate trill of a whippoorwill sounded.

19

Break-in!

*T*he owl and the whippoorwill continued to speak to each other. Two dark-clothed figures moved through the shadows. They came not from the street, not from the alley, but from the yards on either side of the house. They met at the workshop door.

The larger of the two muffled the padlock in a dark scarf and slid a thin wire into it. The lock opened soundlessly. He lifted it from its ring. Slowly he eased the door inward and slipped through the opening. The second figure followed.

Silence reigned. No sound had reached the ears of the sleeping dog in the house.

And so it was that Professor Savvy and Merrill Frobusher entered the workshop.

Inside, working in the dim light of a down-beamed flashlight, they hastily draped the window in black plastic. That done, they stripped off their black caps and gloves.

"Light," said the professor, "if you please."

"Gotcha," said Merrill. He played the flashlight around the workshop until the round beam circled the light switch. He flipped it on.

The room sprang into view.

"I always wondered what was in here," he said, looking around at the workbench and the racks of tools and equipment lining the walls. "But Knockwurst never asked me to come in."

"Hoo-hee!" The professor rubbed his hands gleefully, studying the sheet-swathed object in the center of the room. "What do we have here? And who does the dratted boy think he's hiding things from?" He whipped the sheet off the invention. "Now what can this be! My curiosity bubbles over."

Merrill was doing his own investigating. "Get a load of the tablecloth," he said. "And flowers yet! Knockwurst sure is fancy!"

The professor tore himself away from the giggle

machine and came to stand beside Merrill. A knowing grin spread across his face. "Out of character," he muttered. "Why would there be a fancy tablecloth here?" He lifted the flowers and flipped the cloth aside. "Obviously to hide something!"

The invention safe stood revealed, heavy, solid, bristling with locks.

"Hoo-ha!" chortled the professor. "And what do all these locks tell me?"

Merrill scratched his head. With this professor guy, you never knew what strange things could happen. "They talk to you?"

"They tell me, my boy," the professor explained, "that this strongbox holds something of great value." He stroked his mustache with a single finger, walking around the safe, eyeing it. "The meaning of the nightly trips from the house becomes clear. Valuable things are brought here each evening."

"Hey! Let's open it," said Merrill. "Let's see what's in there."

"My thought exactly," said the professor. "You become more like me each day, my boy."

Merrill looked proud.

The professor knelt and examined the locks. One by one they yielded to his bit of wire. He laid them on the floor, all five of them. Swinging the door wide, he reached inside.

Suddenly he seemed to remember something. Hurriedly he withdrew his hands. "This is your part of the investigation, my boy. As I explained, you are in charge of anything we might wish to carry away tonight."

Proud of being in charge, Merrill brought things out into the light of the room. The flute with its curious clamps and connections. A thick sheaf of music. A notebook filled with—he dropped it in his excitement, for right there behind it was the va-ROOOM machine.

He sat back on his heels, cradling it in his arms. "Knockwurst's skateboard," he crowed, running his hands along its graceful lines. "He never takes it out. He doesn't deserve to have it if he's only gonna keep it locked up. It needs an expert—like me, King of the Board."

The professor wasn't listening. Turning the flute over and over, he studied the connections. Odd. What could they signify?

He flipped through the music. Had he been musical, he would have heard music in his head by looking at the notes. But he was not musical.

He fluttered the pages of the notebook. Numbers, nothing but numbers! Had he been mathematically gifted, he would have understood that the book held the secret to a little-known natural law. But his understanding of math was sadly limited.

Disappointed, he dropped the things. He had hoped

to find something valuable here. But what value could there be in these odd things? They did not tickle his curiosity. Whereas the invention behind him, in the middle of the room—ah, now that made him nearly ill with curiosity.

He turned back to it, pacing around it, his hands behind his back, frowning. What was it? What did it do? Without doubt it was important.

He studied the fan, peered at the corked jug, poked a finger at the feather, brought his face close to the mirror and drew back, getting its full effect. He read the signs, his lips moving. REMOVE SHOES AND SOCKS. STAND HERE. He examined the control panel, its buttons and switches. ON. OFF. PB—whatever that might mean. MAX. MIN.

He made up his mind. "There is, hoo-ha, only one way to satisfy my curiosity." He knelt and removed his shoes. He wasn't wearing socks.

Still clutching the va-ROOOM machine, Merrill watched him, his mouth slightly open. The professor sure was acting strange.

Professor Savvy stepped onto the foot pads, leaned out—which was very hard to do—and pressed a button, the ON button, he thought.

The giggle machine galloped into action, into max. The fan whirred. Music blared. The cap swung from its cord, unnoticed, voices chattering from the ear-flaps.

132

"Hoo-hee," said the professor, his eyebrows lifting as he felt a peculiar tingling in his feet. "Perhaps I'd better . . . better . . . hee-hec—wait until I . . . until I . . ."

He tried to lean out and touch the OFF button, but of course he could not, for the electronic gates had by now locked in place.

"Oh, deary me," he gasped. "I don't seem able to turn this invention off. Perhaps this test was a . . . ha-ha-ha—mistake. Merrill, my boy . . . hee-hee-hee," he gasped between spasms of laughter, "push the . . . ho-ho . . . push the . . ." He could not tell Merrill what to do.

He hopped straight up, laughing, "Hooooo-heeee!" trying to get away from the wildly tickling foot pads. The feather flicked across his nose. "Ha-ha-ah-choo!" Up and down he went, shaking with laughter, hooting with laughter.

Up ho-ho-ho! Down haw-haw-haw! Up giggle-snort! Down hee-hee-hee!

Gone was the silence of the night.

─────20

In the Dead
of Night

*I*nside the house, eyes snapped open, heads lifted from pillows, covers were tossed aside.

Clinton leaped out of his basket. "Ar-rOOOOOO!"

"Ar-rOOOOOO!" sounded his army.

Little Brother was out of bed running, still half-asleep.

Burton was out in the hall ahead of him with his flashlight.

Down the stairs they tumbled, two steps at a time.

Through the house.

Out the back door, with Clinton dashing ahead of them, barking wildly.

Behind them, the dog chorus continued in the house.

Ahead of them, a dog chorus swelled from the workshop.

Burton flung open the door and took in all that was happening—the giggle machine in maximum operation . . . the professor laughing . . . Merrill clutching the va-ROOOM machine, his eyes round, his chin sagging, frozen where he stood.

Little Brother was the first to speak. "I should've guessed they were the skulkers." His voice was drowned out by the raucous noise. He tugged at Burton's sleeve. "Turn it off," he mouthed.

Burton pressed the panic button.

The giggle machine slowed and stopped. The music faded. But the professor went on hooting with laughter, gasping for air, tears streaming down his cheeks. And Clinton and his army continued their frantic barking.

Burton fumbled in his pajama pocket, found the remote for the growl multiplier, and touched it. Suddenly, the only sound in the workshop came from a single fierce dog.

"Quiet, Clint," Little Brother ordered.

After a few noisy moments to show he meant business, Clinton stopped barking. He bared his teeth instead and, growling deep in his throat, advanced on the professor.

Little Brother grabbed him. "Hold it, Clint. Don't bite. Not yet."

If Burton was anything, he was cool in times of stress. "Listen, professor," he said mildly to the little man who now leaned weakly against the giggle machine, "didn't anybody ever tell you that you shouldn't climb into machines you don't know anything about?

"And you"—he turned to Merrill—"put it down, Frobusher," he said quietly, pointing at the va-ROOOM machine. "Now! Or our dog will . . ."

There was no mistaking his meaning.

Moving slowly, his eyes on Clinton, Merrill stooped and set the va-ROOOM machine on the floor.

Burton turned back to Professor Savvy. He pointed at the things lying in front of the invention safe. "You promised! You gave your word to Miss Doyle that you would never, never take anyone's invention ever again. I saw you write it on the chalkboard. Don't you know when you make a promise you've got to keep it?"

The professor swiped a sleeve across his face to wipe away the tears. "But my boy, you do me an injustice," he quavered. "I have not taken anything. I have kept my promise to our revered teacher. This boy," he pointed at Merrill, "was planning on carrying them away."

"Hey!" yelped Merrill. "You're not gonna pin this on me! You were the one who told me I'd be in charge of the stuff we found here."

The professor looked hurt. "But you had to be, my boy. Don't you see? I could not be in charge because I had given my word to Miss Doyle."

Burton knew flimflam when he heard it. The professor was flimflamming himself and flimflamming Merrill and he was trying to flimflam him, Burton, too.

"You think because Merrill was going to carry the stuff, you weren't taking it?" he said. His voice became hard. "You thought you were keeping your promise to Miss Doyle? Well, you weren't. You were being sneaky. You were—"

"What is the meaning of this?" roared a voice from the doorway.

Standing there was Papa, his baton in his hand. Mama stood beside him, armed with a rolling pin.

Burton and Little Brother looked at them in awe. This was a Papa and Mama they did not know. Papa's face was magenta. Mama's eyes were steely.

The professor turned pale.

"We demand an explanation," said Mama in an icy voice.

"Uh—hoo-hee—uh—er—" The professor was unable to speak.

Papa and Mama advanced into the workshop. Edisonia peeked in from the doorway.

"Speak," thundered Papa.

"At once," snapped Mama.

The professor licked his lips. A wily look replaced the confusion on his face. "Good evening, madam, sir." His tones dripped honey. "I am honored to meet the esteemed heads of the Knockwurst family. I am, myself, Professor Savvy." He held out his hand.

"Enough!" roared Papa, and he brought his baton down on the hand. *Thwack!*

The Professor jumped back, rubbing it.

"What are you doing here in the dead of night, inside this workshop, having broken into that"—Mama pointed with the rolling pin—"safe?"

"I was driven," whined the professor. "The curiosity of a questing mind led me here. I was merely trying to satisfy my considerable curiosity about the wondrous things going on here." He turned to Burton. "This amazing machine, for instance. What can be its purpose? Perhaps you would share a bit of information with a colleague?"

Papa pointed at the door with his baton. "You, sir, are a scoundrel and a nincompoop. Never darken our door again."

"Leave," Mama commanded, "before I am forced to use this weapon."

The professor moved fast on his bare feet. He darted toward the door. "Of course, sir. Certainly, madam. Anything you say, gentle people."

139

"Wait for me," wailed Merrill. "Don't leave me here."

"It's every man for himself, lad," called the professor as he disappeared into the darkness.

"Go on, Merrill. Get lost," said Burton, "while the going's good."

Merrill shot across the workshop and out the door.

Little Brother hung on to Clinton with both hands. "It's okay, boy," he said soothingly. "Papa and Mama are looking after things. Calm down, boy. The bad guys are gone."

Applause sounded from the doorway. Edisonia was clapping her hands. "Bravo, Papa! Brava, Mama. You were simply wonderful!"

Papa and Mama looked surprised, and then they looked shyly pleased, and then they looked—like Papa and Mama once more.

"It is very late at night," said Papa, "for young people to be up and about."

"Goodness me, yes," Mama agreed. "Come indoors, dears. We'll have a little sip of something to unwind after all this excitement."

Papa scooped up his music and headed for the house.

Mama smoothed the pages of her notebook and followed him.

Edisonia, polishing her flute on the hem of her nightie, trailed after them.

Burton disconnected the key parts of the giggle machine so that nobody could turn it on when he wasn't there. He checked over the va-ROOOM machine to be sure it had not been damaged and tucked it under his arm. Tonight it would stay with him, safely under his bed.

Clinton eyed the shoes lying beside the giggle machine. He did not like those shoes. He pounced, growling, and started chewing on the nearest one.

Little Brother turned off the light. "Come on, Clint," he said. "Come on, boy."

He closed the door. Tomorrow he would get a combination lock and learn the numbers by heart and never tell them to anyone but Burton. Nobody would be able to get past that kind of lock.

With Clinton tagging after him, Professor Savvy's shoe in his mouth, Little Brother followed his family into the house.

21 ―――――――――

A Letter for
Little Brother

*L*ittle Brother had just had a spine-chilling idea. "Now that Professor Savvy has been in the giggle machine, maybe he'll feel so good that he'll solve his problems. I mean, maybe he'll figure out how to take what he wants from the workshop."

Burton considered the thought. Then he began to smile. "Think back to how things looked when we went into the workshop."

"The giggle machine was running at max," said Little Brother, frowning, remembering, "and he was laughing so hard he could hardly breathe. And—and—" He suddenly remembered. "The cork was still in the ion jug!"

"Right," said Burton. "He didn't get any of the risible ions. While all the other things were good, by themselves they couldn't really happify the professor."

"The laugh ions—they're what makes the difference," said Little Brother. "Wasn't it lucky I read about those in that magazine!"

They were sitting around the fireplace, winding down from the excitement of the past hour, sipping mulled carrot juice topped with marshmallows. Between sips, Edisonia played whisper-soft woodsy-sounding melodies on her flute.

Clinton had his own treat. He lay close to the fire chomping happily on the professor's right shoe.

"And anyway," Burton continued, "I think Papa threw a real scare into the professor. I don't think we have to worry about him coming back." He looked at Papa and Mama, relaxing in their cozy armchairs, smiling gently. Who would believe that they could be so fierce!

Suddenly Mama looked up at the mantelpiece and remembered something. "Little Brother, pet—"

Little Brother sighed at the babyish name.

"—a letter came for you today. I forgot all about it. It's up there on the mantel."

Little Brother leaped up. The letter he had been waiting for! At last! He tore it open.

"But why ever is the government writing to you?" asked Mama.

Little Brother was reading the letter. A slow grin spread across his face. He handed the letter to Burton.

Burton read it and looked up at him wonderingly. "It says the va-ROOOM machine is registered in my name."

"Wonderful!" exclaimed Papa. "That means even if somebody whose name we will not mention makes another like it—"

"It would be against the law. The government knows

144

that Burton invented it," said Little Brother. "They'd be mad at Professor Savvy."

Clinton looked up from the tattered shoe. "Grrr," he growled.

Edisonia shuddered. "I wouldn't want the government to be mad at me." Then she thought of something else. "How did you know about doing that?"

"Read about it in the library," said Little Brother, licking delicious gooey marshmallow off his upper lip.

"And can you tell the government about my harp-flute?" asked Edisonia.

"Yep," said Little Brother. "Now that I know how to do it."

Edisonia smiled, pleased, and started another wispy-sounding air on her flute.

"So that's why you wanted my drawings of the va-ROOOM machine," said Burton.

"I sent them to Washington," said Little Brother.

"And that's why you made me promise not to go out on the va-ROOOM machine for a while," said Burton.

"Well, see," Little Brother said seriously, "I didn't know if the government would do it, and I thought we ought to wait and see."

"Tomorrow morning," said Burton, "I'm going to take it out for a spin and it doesn't matter if anyone sees it." He thought of something. Little Brother had done a wonderful thing. He deserved a reward. "Listen," he said, "Little Brother—I mean Newton—would you like me to make a va-ROOOM machine for you, too?"

"Would I!" exclaimed Little Brother. "Oh, would I!"

Burton was thoughtful. "You know, I might make them for the kids, too. We could have a regular flying squadron. But you," he said to Little Brother—Newton—"you would be first officer, of course."

Stars shone in Little Brother's eyes. Never, *never*, had he felt like such a big kid!

Burton sat quietly, sipping his mulled carrot juice, sleepy and contented, thinking about the va-ROOOM machine and the flying squadron and the giggle machine.

The giggle machine. It had helped Tish and Jonathan and Kevin. They had gone from being unhappy to being hopeful and had found the answers to their terrible troubles. The giggle machine had done exactly what he intended.

On the other hand—he frowned—it had done something he had not known it would do. It had trapped the professor. Because he had not meant that to happen, it was, in a way, a glitch. He wasn't going to be a really top-notch inventor until there were no glitches of any kind in his inventions. He was, he promised himself, going to work on that.

Then he remembered Professor Savvy, laughing wildly, and he grinned. He thought of the little man caving in before stern Papa and Mama, and his grin broadened. The glitch had been a good one. He should not argue with himself about good glitches!

He downed the rest of his mulled carrot juice. He yawned and stretched. Bedtime. Tomorrow was another day. Who knew what wonderful inventions were out there just waiting to be thought of?

About the Author

DOROTHY HAAS is a former children's book editor. She lives in Chicago, Illinois, where she is now a full-time writer. She is also the author of *Burton's Zoom Zoom Va-Rooom Machine.*

Let
Bruce Coville
take you to the **Magic Shop** –
where adventure begins!

THE MONSTER'S RING
Illustrated by Katherine Coville

JEREMY THATCHER, DRAGON HATCHER
Illustrated by Gary A. Lippincott

JENNIFER MURDLEY'S TOAD
Illustrated by Gary A. Lippincott